"Flowers and pups, love and miracles... and robust faith that answers unasked questions and overshadows every fear. Vickie Fisher has outdone herself with Tulips of Love. My advice to you? Make room on your "keepers shelf" for this one, because it's sure to be one you'll read again. And again!

—*LOREE LOUGH, bestselling author of 119 award-winning novels, including reader favorites like* 50 Hours *and* A Man of Honor

"This powerful story takes you inside the trials and triumphs created by a family illness, enlightening your spirit. For anyone who believes in the power of God, a must read!"

—*CONNIE C. SCHARON, Amazon best-selling author of* Enchanted Lover

TULIPS
of Love

VICKIE FISHER

Print ISBN: 978-1-7373842-0-5
Ebook ISBN: 978-1-7373842-1-2

Cover design by PixelStudio

This book is a work of fiction. All characters except for the spiritual hero are fictitious. If you happen to see your name, then thank you for having such an awesome name, but the character is a figment of the author's imagination.

Scripture verses are taken from the King James, New International, and English Standard Versions of the Bible.

To learn more about the author check out her website at: vickiefisher.com.

Dedication

To my children and grandchildren.
I am truly blessed.

Acknowledgments

First and foremost I have to acknowledge God, for creating within me the love of writing. For Your son Jesus, without Him, nothing would be worthwhile.

To my editor and publisher Demi Stevens and Year of the Book. Your magical touch took *Tulips of Love* to the next level.

Thanks to my nieces Ashley Eckard and Carrie Yost for helping me with my healthcare questions.

A special thanks to Carol Silvis, Connie Scharon, Luke Fisher, Loree Lough, and Megan Davis. You make me a better writer. Thanks for being on my team.

Chapter 1

The veil between dreams and reality began to lift. Jeff sank farther beneath the down comforter. He reached across the bed for his wife, but came up with a handful of air. He sighed. *No cuddling this morning.*

The aroma of brewing coffee drifted up the stairs. He stretched then rolled out of bed. Through the window, he could see the sun just peeking over the horizon, casting its ray of light on the hill behind the house. Jeff smiled. The tulips were in full bloom. Which meant today was Tulip of Love Day.

Michelle believed tulips were God's first visible sign of love. He agreed. This had been an extra-long winter and the flowers were a welcome relief. He pulled on a pair of jeans and a flannel shirt.

At the top of the stairs he glanced into Jack's room. His son was still sleeping soundly. Jeff whispered to the dog to come. Shadow lifted his head before putting it back down. "I see how it is." It was amazing how loyal that dog was to Jack. He would not move until the child was up.

Jeff hurried down the stairs. Once the kids realized what today was, there would be no more quiet time.

Entering the dark empty kitchen, he flipped on the light. Michelle was standing with her head leaning against the French doors in the family room. She flinched and squeezed her eyes shut.

He quickly turned the switch back off, then slipped up behind her and kissed her neck. "Sorry about the light. Another headache?"

She barely nodded. "The cold glass feels good against my head." She moved, letting the lace curtains fall back into place. Her attempt at a smile was more of a grimace. She added, "The tulips are blooming."

"Woohoo," their daughter Beth shouted as the nine year old ran to their side. "Can I see?"

"You know the rules," Jeff said. "No peeking until we are all here."

Running out of the room, Beth yelled, "Jack, it's Tulip of Love Day." They could hear her as she dashed up the stairs and into her brother's room.

"You would think it was Christmas or something the way you people act about those silly tulips," Jeff said.

"Silly tulips, *hmph.*" Michelle put the bacon in the oven, slowly turning her head to look over her shoulder at him. "You can't fool me. I know you're looking forward to it as much as we are." She handed him a mug of coffee. "Besides baseball practice with Jack, do we have any other plans for the day?"

He followed her into the kitchen. "You know I can cook breakfast if you want to go lie down until the headache goes away."

"Thanks, but it's really not too bad. Just a little one."

"I don't know... you look pale. I bet sometimes even the virtuous woman had help."

Michelle smirked. "You can help by keeping the kids quiet." She stirred the pancake mix. "Anyway I don't think you can make tulip pancakes, can you?"

"Maybe not as pretty as yours." He winked. "But they would be something to talk about for years to come."

The kids burst into the kitchen, followed by their Siberian husky Shadow. "Can we go outside now?" they asked.

"Inside voices," Jeff said, raising a finger to his lips.

Beth lowered her voice to almost a whisper and repeated, "Can we?"

Michelle took a sip of hot tea. "It's chilly this morning. Go get your jackets."

"This year there will be more tulips than ever," Beth said. "I can't wait to see the pink ones I planted."

"And I planted orange ones for the Orioles, right Dad?"

"You sure did."

Michelle stood with her hands on the French doors. "Are we ready?"

"Yes!" shouted Beth and Jack.

With a flourish Michelle flung open the doors. "It's Tulip of Love Day."

The kids ran out, stopping in awe at the sight of the hill half covered in tulips of every color. Shadow barked and raced past them. Michelle stood for a moment, admiring the breathtaking view.

"Wow, we've had a lot of blessings, haven't we, Mom?"

"We sure have." Michelle stooped down to hug her children to her. "It has been a long winter, and God is showing us His love with the beauty of the tulips." She gave them a gentle push. "Now go pick one of your favorites so we can put them on the table as a reminder... not only of our blessings this year, but of God's wonderful love."

Beth ran straight to a pink one and Jack to an orange one.

Jeff put his arm around his wife. "Do I need to ask what color you want?"

"You know I'm going for a red one." She nudged him and asked, "What about you?"

"Red, of course."

They held hands as they climbed the flagstone path. Halfway up, the path veered off, only to rejoin, forming a heart filled with red tulips. Leaning in, he picked the one in the center. "This was the tulip that started it all. What a wonderful blessing this flower has brought us." He pulled her to him. "I love you," he whispered as he joined his lips to hers.

"Oh no, they're kissing," Jack said, covering his eyes.

Beth ran behind them and wrapped her arms as wide as she could around their waists.

Jeff reached down and swooped her up with one arm. He kissed her cheek, then his wife's. "My two favorite girls," he said and hugged them tight.

Beth giggled, "I love Tulip of Love Day."

Jeff winked at Michelle before releasing his arm from around her. He grabbed hold of Beth's waist and tossed her in the air. "So do I, buttercup." Laughing he put her down and reached for Jack, tossing him into the air next. When Jack was back on the ground, Jeff grabbed Michelle by the hands.

She started to pull away. "You are not going to toss me!"

He laughed, "No," then pulled her close and started two-stepping around the flagstone path.

Beth skipped behind them while Jack ran ahead. Shadow yelped and ran from one to the other. But when they headed into the downward part of the path, Jeff felt Michelle stumble. He scooped her into his arms without a second thought and continued dancing up and down the hill with the kids and Shadow parading behind.

"You can put me down now," Michelle said.

He whispered, "Is this bothering your headache?"

"No."

"Then I'm not putting you down. Any chance I get to hold you in my arms is one I'm not giving up."

She kissed his cheek. "I love you so much."

He grinned at the kids. "Want to hear the tulip story?"

They both clapped, jumping up and down. "Yes."

"Once upon a time there was a handsome prince who wanted to buy the only red tulip at the store."

Michelle giggled, "Handsome prince, huh?" He put her feet on the ground but didn't let go of her.

"That is what the beautiful princess said." Jeff winked at her.

Beth started to giggle. "I love this story."

Jeff continued, "Just as his hand touched the potted tulip, another hand landed on it. Now the prince could tell by the dainty fingers with red nail polish, he would have no trouble taking the tulip as his own. Until he lifted his gaze and looked into the most beautiful blue eyes he had ever seen. Then he knew he would willingly give not only the coveted tulip to her... but the world, if he could."

Michelle whispered in his ear, "You are so silly."

"Now he wasn't going to just *give* the beautiful princess the flower, for fear if he let go of the pot, she would disappear and he would never find her again. So he quickly said, 'I will buy you the tulip, but only if you go for coffee with me'." He nodded toward his daughter.

Beth, imitating her mother, said, "I don't drink coffee."

Jeff nodded at Jack next and the little boy said, "Well, the place has other things to drink besides coffee."

Beth pushed her brother. "He didn't say that."

Jack put his hands on his hips. "Well, he should have. She was just being difficult."

Michelle and Jeff tried not to laugh.

"She was not," Beth argued. "She was being careful. She didn't know him."

"Okay, let me finish the story," Jeff interrupted. "The difficult princess—" Michelle busted out laughing. Jeff rolled his eyes at her and continued. "The princess said, 'I don't drink coffee.' And the prince, being full of patience said, 'You can order whatever you would like.' Suddenly she smiled at the prince and from that moment on he has never been the same. Six months later they were married, and they planted the bulb of their first tulip. When it bloomed the next year it looked so lonely on this big hill. That is when the princess came up with the brilliant idea to plant a tulip for each of their blessings." He spread his arms out. "Ten years later we have a garden of love."

"That is the best story ever," Beth said, hugging both of her parents.

"Isn't it amazing how God can take something as simple as a flower and turn it into a lifetime of love?" Michelle kissed her children before reaching up and kissing Jeff. "My handsome prince," she said with a grin. "So tell us your blessings."

Jack pointed. "That orange one is 'cause the Orioles made the playoffs last year."

"I planted the pink ones because I made honor roll," Beth said.

Michelle pointed at a variegated pink and yellow tulip. "I planted that one because I have been blessed with the two greatest kids on the planet."

Jeff pointed to the red tulips. "Your mother and I planted these two for another year together." He pointed to the center of the heart. "Look at all those red tulips. I bet there are at least forty... and yet we have only planted nineteen of them. One the first year, and two for each of the years we have been married." He bent down, picked three red tulips, and handed one to Michelle. "When I married you, I never thought I could love you more. I was wrong. My love for you has multiplied beyond words..." He gave a tulip each to Beth and Jack.

"...and has given us the wonderful gift of you two. We plant these flowers as a reminder of our blessings every year. I find it amazing that as our love multiplies, so do the tulips. It won't be long before this heart is overflowing, like my heart is with love for the three of you."

Beth and Jack flung their arms around their parents, almost knocking them down. Jeff's arms went around his family. He gently collapsed with them to the ground, making sure he landed on the top of the pile, and started tickling them. The children's laughter was music to his ears.

Somehow, Michelle inched away and suddenly she was on top tickling him. "Come on, kids. Let's get him."

"I give," Jeff said between the laughing. He stood, pulling the kids up with him. He then held out a hand to Michelle, helping her stand.

She brushed the dirt from her pants and said, "I'm hungry, how about you?"

"Are we having tulip pancakes?" Jack asked.

"Of course," Michelle answered ruffling his hair. "Why don't you each pick me one more flower so we can have tulip tea?"

Jeff made a face.

Michelle laughed. "Don't worry. You can have *coffee.*"

"*Phew,*" he whispered in her ear. "I don't like tulip tea."

"I know."

Jeff bent down to pick some of the red tulips for the table.

Back inside, Michelle said, "My handsome prince, would you get the vase from the top shelf in the pantry? Jack and Beth, go wash your hands so you can help me."

"Mommy, can I get the tulip teapot and cups?" Michelle looked at her daughter. "I'm nine. Not a little girl anymore," Beth said. "I know to be very careful."

"Yes. And how about you make the tea?"

Beth clasped her hands together. "Thank you, thank you." She ran to the china cabinet, and with care she picked up the red tulip teapot, then carried it to the kitchen island before going back for the cups.

Jeff noticed Michelle couldn't keep from smiling as she watched Beth softly place each tulip cup on its saucer at each of their place settings on the table. Her hand lingered a moment on the handles. With a big grin she said, "Time to make the tea." Beth hurried around the island. Picking up the tulips she asked, "What do I do first?"

"You wash them."

"Yes, please do," Jack said. "I don't want bird poo in my tea."

"Oh, Jack." Beth rolled her eyes at him.

"After you gently wash them, pat them dry, then bring them over here." Together Michelle and Beth pulled the petals off the flowers, and put them into the teapot. Michelle picked up the whistling kettle, now filled with hot water. Jeff could see her hand shaking and made a move to help.

Putting the pot back down, she immediately said, "Beth, would you like to pour the water into the tulip teapot this year?"

Beth grinned, then slowly poured the hot water over the tulip petals and put the lid on top.

"Great job." Michelle rubbed her daughter's back. "By the time the pancakes are finished, the tea will be, too. Would you run and get our blessings book from the desk so we can read it and remember why we planted the tulips?" She turned back to the stove, carefully pouring each pancake into the shape of a tulip.

Jeff watched closely. Her hands were no longer trembling. "It's amazing how you can do that."

"Years of practice." She grinned. "Remember how they looked that first year?"

Jeff winked. "Oh, were those supposed to have been tulips?" He chuckled when she swatted him. "They were very lovely."

"*Hmm.*" She handed him the plate of bacon and said, "You can set this on the table." Then she followed him with the pancakes.

After they said grace, Michelle started to pour the tea. Jack put his small hand over his cup. "I don't like tulip tea."

"You have to drink it, Jack," Beth added. "It's *tradition.*"

"Daddy doesn't drink it," Jack argued. "So I don't have to either." He pulled his shoulders back. "We men don't drink sissy drinks."

Jeff saw the disappointment flash in his wife's eyes and held out his cup to her. "Of course I'm going to drink the tea." Her radiant smile was all the reward he needed, but he was glad when she only filled his cup halfway. "It *is* tradition... and with lots of honey, I'm sure it will be delicious."

Michelle kissed his cheek and whispered, "You are the best."

He winked and said, "I know," and held out Jack's cup to be filled.

"But—"

"Men do what needs to be done to make the women we love happy." Jeff poured lots of honey into Jack's tea and stirred. When everyone had their cups in hand, Jeff picked up his own, making a toast with Jack. "Sometimes we have to take one for the team." Jeff took a sip of his tea, trying to keep his face straight. "Umm, yummy."

"Yuck," Jack said.

Michelle and Beth drank from their cups as if it was the most delicious tea ever. Over tulip pancakes and bacon, they talked about all the blessings they'd had that year.

Chapter 2

"Looks like we are the first ones here," Jeff said as they pulled to a stop in front of the baseball field.

"As always," Michelle replied.

"The coach has to be on time."

Jeff had barely put the truck in park before Jack and Beth hopped out of the Silverado and took off running.

"Hey, you two," Jeff called after them. "You aren't getting off that easy." He pointed to the equipment he was pulling from the back of the truck.

"Oh, man." Jack ran back.

Other cars started to arrive. "Mr. Stevens, you need any help?" one of the boys asked. Together with his friends, Jack and the boys made quick work of carrying the gear down to the field.

Michelle grabbed one of the folding chairs and asked, "Beth, are you going to need a chair?"

"Not yet, Mommy," she said as she linked arms with her cousin Kim. "We're going to the playground." Together they skipped away, giggling as they sang a silly song.

Michelle nodded, but the slight movement sent pain shooting through her head. She grabbed the tailgate, waiting for the throbbing to stop.

Jeff put his arm around her. "Are you okay?"

"Yes."

Jeff took the lawn chair from her and set it up in her normal spot at the top of the hill. From there she could watch the boys practicing yet still see Beth at the playground. Before heading down to the field, he kissed the top of her head and said, "Let me know if you need me."

"I'm fine," she lied and inwardly rejoiced when her sister walked across the parking lot.

Annette opened her folding chair beside Michelle. "Looks like we finally have a good day for baseball."

"Thank goodness," Michelle said. "I thought this was supposed to be a warm weather sport."

"So did I." Annette placed a thermos of hot chocolate beside her chair. "Something to warm us if we need it. The sun might feel good, but the air is still chilly."

Michelle patted the blanket hanging on the back of her own chair. "Yep. Just in case." They laughed.

Annette glanced across the field. "Looks like we're going to have another good team." Her husband Blake was the assistant coach. "The kids are lucky they have those two," she said pointing to Blake and Jeff.

Michelle nodded slightly, but it made her head pulsate with pain. Instinctively, her hand flew to her forehead, pressing in.

"You okay?"

"Another headache."

"You ought to have Blake check you out," Annette said.

"Doctor or not, your husband will not be examining me."

Annette laughed. "It's just your head."

"First the head, then who knows what." This made them both giggle.

Annette reached into her purse and asked, "Want some Advil?"

"I've taken something already."

"Hi!" Helen, the mother of one of the boys, stopped in front of them. She shuffled her feet and fiddled with her hands.

"Helen," Michelle looked up, trying to smile. "It's nice to see you."

"I was wondering if you could give Timmy a ride to practice on Monday." The woman looked down at the ground. "I hate to ask, but you did say if he ever needed a ride—"

"Of course," Michelle soothed. "We will gladly pick him up."

"Oh, thank you. I have to work late." Helen softly chuckled. "I know he isn't very good, but he does love playing."

It was all Michelle could do to stand up and place her hand on Helen's arm. "In no time at all, Jeff and Blake will have him playing like all the other boys."

Helen's face lit up. "You think so?"

"I *know* so."

Helen said thank you before dashing off after her toddler.

Michelle gingerly sat back down.

Annette laughed and pointed over to the playground. "Look at Beth and Kimmy trying to do cartwheels."

Michelle turned her head to see, but she couldn't seem to focus. Her vision was blurry. Minutes later she started to feel nauseous and clutched her stomach. Pushing down on the arms of the chair, she tried to stand, but fell roughly backward.

"Are you okay?" her sister asked, but didn't wait for a response. Annette was up and out of her chair, kneeling in front of Michelle.

With a hand still to her stomach, Michelle whispered, "Would you mind taking me home? I'm not feeling well."

Annette shot up. "Definitely. Let me go get Beth." She was halfway to the playground before getting the girls' attention. They ran to her. "Your mom's not feeling good, so I'm taking her home." She gently squeezed Beth's shoulder. "Get your stuff so we can leave."

Beth begged to be left playing with her cousin Kimmy. "I can come home with Dad," she whined.

"Okay," Annette agreed, "but before we leave, you have to run down and tell him what's going on. I'll wait here until you do."

Beth ran to the fence and called to her father. Michelle saw him glance up to her spot on the hill, then race up beside her. "I'll take you home." He knelt down in front of her chair, taking her hands in his.

"No, the kids need you here," Michelle argued.

"You need me more."

"I just need to lay down. There's nothing you can do for me." She pointed to the field. "You are needed here."

"But—"

Annette put a hand on his shoulder. "I'll make sure she's tucked in."

Jeff kissed the top of Michelle's head. "Okay. But call me if you need me."

Pulling out of the parking lot, Annette said, "Good thing we're close to home. You don't look good."

Michelle laid her head against the window and mumbled, "I-on't-ee-go…"

"What?"

The words came out of Michelle's mouth in a jumbled mess. She felt darkness slipping over her.

Jeff's cell phone rang. He unclicked it from his side. His heart beat faster when he saw Annette's name. She was sobbing, "Jeff, Michelle had a seizure. She's lost consciousness."

"*What?*" Jeff's voice rose in panic.

"Gamber EMTs are here and they're taking her to the hospital."

He heard his sister-in-law's voice, but couldn't comprehend what she was talking about. "Seizure? Where are you?"

"By Cindy Lane."

"I'll be right there," he said and raced across the field.

"No, meet us at the hospital," Annette insisted. "The ambulance should be pulling out soon."

Jeff quickly told Blake what was happening and ran toward his SUV.

Beth came running. "What's the matter?"

"It's Mommy. She got sick. I have to go." He fumbled in his pocket for the key fob. "Uncle Blake will bring you home." With the remote now in hand, he gave Beth a tight hug. "Mommy's going to be fine." The sound of an ambulance speeding by brought him back to the moment. "I have to go."

A look of panic sped across Beth's face. "Is Mommy in that ambulance?"

"She's fine, buttercup." He knelt down beside her and with more conviction than he felt, said, "Let's pray."

Before Jeff could even get out another word, he saw his son running toward them. "What's happening, Daddy?"

"I need to get going. Mommy got sick, and I have to go be with her. We are going to pray for her, then I have to go." Jeff put his arms around both of his children. "Dear Heavenly Father, we lift our wife and mother, Michelle, up to you. We ask that you place your hand upon her head and remove her pain. Please also watch over Beth and Jack, and help them not to worry. We love and trust You to do Your will. Amen." He wiped their tears. "It will be okay. Mommy is in God's hands." Jeff hugged them and turned Jack back to the field. "Your team is waiting for you." To Beth he said, "I'm going to call Grandma. She'll be here soon."

With that, he jumped in the SUV, throwing up gravel as he sped off. He glanced in the rearview mirror and saw his children staring after him. His heart clenched in his chest. He was grateful when one of the other mothers walked up and put her arms around them. Jeff quickly dialed the number for his mother-in-law. She would calm their fears.

It took all his willpower not to lay on the horn when he got behind a slow driver. Forcing a deep breath, Jeff tried to calm the pounding of his heart. He reminded himself God was in control.

After what seemed like a lifetime he raced into the emergency room. Before the double sliding doors were fully open, Jeff breathlessly shouted, "My wife was just brought in—Michelle Stevens."

"They are working on her now," a woman behind the desk said. "As soon as I can, I will send you back."

Jeff stared at the oversized door blocking him from Michelle. It might as well have been a concrete wall. A hand touched his arm. "It happened so fast." Tears were streaming down Annette's face. Jeff put his arm around her. "She couldn't talk then…" she sobbed into his chest. "I'm so scared."

Jeff whispered, "Me too."

"I can take you back now, Mr. Stevens," a nurse prompted from the double doors.

Jeff and Annette followed her to a small room. His heart almost stopped. Annette let out an involuntary gasp. Michelle's face was as pale as the sheets. A heart monitor and IV were attached to her.

Another nurse looked up at him and said, "She's back with us, but she's still very disoriented." The woman motioned for them to come in.

Jeff hurried to his wife's side, and softly whispered her name.

Michelle slowly opened her eyes, looking toward him with a blank stare. She blinked a few times.

He reached for her hand.

She whispered, "Where am I?"

Jeff leaned over and kissed her forehead. "In the hospital."

Annette patted her sister's hand.

A doctor came bustling in and asked, "Mrs. Stevens, can you tell me what happened?"

Michelle shook her head ever so slightly. She looked between Jeff and Annette. "Maybe they can."

"Tell me the last thing you remember."

Michelle rubbed her head. "I had a headache... we were getting ready for baseball practice." She looked at Jeff. "The practice?"

"Blake has it covered."

"The kids?"

"Your parents."

"So you were getting ready..." the doctor prompted.

"I don't remember anything else."

"You don't remember being at the field?" Annette asked.

Michelle looked puzzled. "I was at the field?"

The doctor stepped up to the bed. "I need to do a quick exam to see what might be going on."

Jeff and Annette stepped back.

When he was finished the doctor said, "I'm going to order a CAT scan. We need to know what caused this seizure."

"A seizure?" Michelle whispered in shock.

Ten minutes later an orderly came in and prepared to push the gurney out into the hall.

"Can we go with her?" Jeff asked the doctor.

"Yes, but just to the door of the x-ray room. You will have to sit in the waiting room while she's inside."

Jeff nodded. He held his wife's hand as the orderly wheeled her down the hall.

Annette kissed her cheek. "Practice ought to be over. I'll go get the kids so Blake can come check on you."

"He's not examining me." Michelle and Annette attempted a giggle, but fell short of a sob.

Just fifteen minutes after the orderly wheeled Michelle back to her room, the doctor returned. "We're going to admit you," he said.

"Why?" Michelle asked.

Jeff instinctively reached for his wife's hand. "What did the CAT scan show?"

"There is an abnormality." The doctor turned his laptop around to show them and pointed to a mass on the screen. "I have ordered an MRI so we can get a better look."

"That looks big," Jeff said in alarm.

"I have a call in to Dr. Carson." The doctor avoided giving a direct response. "He's already at the hospital so he'll be in soon to talk to you." Before leaving, the doctor said, "The nurse will be back in to get you."

Michelle squeezed her eyes shut. Jeff sat on the edge of the bed and pulled her into his arms. She whispered into his chest, "It's nothing to worry about." She choked on her next words, "G-God has this."

Her shoulders shook as she tried to hold back the tears. Michelle held onto her husband a few more minutes. She pulled back, placing a kiss on Jeff's cheek before leaning back on the pillows.

"I wonder if Dr. Carson is Jennifer Carson's husband."

"He is," said a tall handsome man in the doorway. Holding out a hand toward Michelle, he continued, "I take it you know my wife."

"Yes, from church." Michelle accepted his hand. "Nice to finally meet you."

The two of them chatted together a few minutes about Jennifer before Dr. Carson mentioned getting a call from Blake.

Jeff interrupted, "Doctor, please." He squeezed Michelle's hand and asked, "Why did this happen? What is that mass in her head?" Questions one after another spilled out of Jeff.

Dr. Carson laid a hand on Jeff's shoulder. "After the MRI, I'll know more about how to answer your questions." He patted Michelle's leg. "I understand you have already been examined a few times. But now it's my turn." He pulled out his retinoscope and looked into her eyes.

It was late when Michelle was finally taken to a room. Jeff slumped down on the chair beside her bed.

"You need to go home," she said. "The kids will be worried sick."

"They're with your parents. I'm sure your dad has Jack in the workshop, and your mother probably has Beth baking something for you when you get home."

"But—"

"No buts. I'm not leaving you."

"They need you."

Jeff leaned onto the bed, cupping her hands in his. "I c-can't leave you." His voice cracked. He gently kissed her lips. "The kids are fine and I need to be here with you." He sat on the bed beside her. "Dr. Carson said he would be in soon… We can call the kids after that." He squeezed her hand. "Okay?"

She nodded before laying her head on his shoulder.

Dr. Carson was not smiling when he knocked and entered the room later. He opened his laptop and turned it so they could see. "I'm afraid I don't have good news for you. The abnormality we saw in the CAT scan is a tumor."

Michelle and Jeff both gasped.

"A tumor." Jeff sagged on the bed, putting his arm around Michelle's shoulders and pulling her to his side.

"I am going to schedule you for a biopsy tomorrow morning."

"A biopsy?" they both said at once. Michelle placed her hand to the side of her head.

"How is that possible?" Jeff asked.

Dr. Carson's words were slow and carefully selected. "I will drill a small hole in the skull and extract a tiny piece of the tumor."

Michelle touched her head. "Will you be shaving my head?"

"No," he chuckled. "The hole will be so small I can just part your hair."

Jeff felt her breathe a sigh of relief.

"I ordered them to give you dinner," Dr. Carson said, "but you aren't to eat or drink anything after ten o'clock. Okay?"

They stared at Dr. Carson's back as he walked out of the room. Seconds passed into minutes. Finally Michelle whispered, "I'm scared."

Blood rushed to Jeff's ears. He fought for control and said, "I know, baby, so am I." He crawled into the bed beside her, put his arm around her shoulders, and pulled her to him. "We have nothing to fear." He kissed the top of her head and added, "You are in good hands—God's and the doctor's." He tried to smile.

Chapter 3

It was late Monday afternoon before Michelle was finally released from the hospital. They rode home in stunned silence. Jeff held her hand tightly in his.

"It will—" he started to say.

"Don't say it," Michelle interrupted. She squeezed his hand and stared out the window, watching the countryside fly by. Her heart ached knowing this might very well be her last ride home. Her stomach flipped when they pulled into the long driveway. Each bump in the road jolted her nerves.

When Jeff pulled up in front of their Victorian farmhouse, the door flew open and the kids ran out screaming, "Mommy, you're home!" The dog ran behind, barking.

Tears welled in Michelle's eyes. She put her hands over her face, willing this nightmare away. She watched her children getting closer. "We have to tell them." She choked back tears.

"I don't know." Jeff reached for her hand and gripped it tight.

"It wouldn't be fair for them not to know."

"We'll tell them in a few days."

"No, we need to tell them now. You heard the doctor." She laid a hand to her head. "My brain is a literal ticking time bomb." She bit her lower lip. "They need to know."

Beth and Jack reached the car. Michelle put a smile on her face and opened the door. "Time to be brave."

She barely made it out of the vehicle before the kids engulfed her in a hug. "We missed you!"

She knelt down and pulled them into her arms. Holding them tight she said, "I missed you, too," then kissed them each on the cheek. Shadow almost knocked her over. Michelle patted the dog's head. "I missed you, too, boy."

Jeff gave Michelle his hand, helping her up. "Let's go inside. Mommy still needs her rest."

"What's wrong?" Beth asked

"Are you okay?" Jack said.

"We'll talk about it inside." Michelle glanced to the doorway and saw her parents standing there. Another sob broke from her throat.

Jeff pulled her close. "We got this." He pointed to the sky. "God has this."

Michelle nodded, took a deep breath, and headed toward the house.

Once inside the foyer, everyone surrounded Michelle and started talking at once. Frank, Michelle's dad, let out a loud whistle. "One at a time."

"Thanks, Dad." Michelle giggled. "Just what my headache needed."

He pulled her into his arms. "Sorry, baby girl."

"I was only teasing. I actually don't have a headache today."

Her mother, Kay, clasped her hands together. "Great, they were able to find the problem and fix it?"

"Let's all go into the family room where we can talk," Jeff said. The kids took off running, followed by the others.

Michelle looked around her, as if for the last time. She smiled at the padded bench in front of the window. Beth and Jack's shoes were under it, where they belonged for a change. She glanced up the staircase... photos of their life lined the wall—their wedding portrait, Beth's first ballet, Jack playing baseball, and her favorite picture of them all sitting among the tulips. Her eyes fell on the picture of Jesus in the center of the family photographs. She silently cried, *Why?* She knew this time there would be no answer.

I know it's not always for me to understand, but to have faith anyway. And I do, but right now I could use an extra dose. Michelle closed her eyes. *Help me through this.*

She put her hands on the foyer table for support, nearly knocking over a vase of tulips. The beauty of the bouquet filled her with renewed hope. Michelle took a deep breath, filling herself with strength from their blessings. She looked up to see Jeff watching her. She smiled and whispered, "We got this."

Shadow brushed her legs and she petted the dog's head. They walked into the kitchen, Shadow almost sliding across the tile floor in his hurry to get to Jack. She couldn't help but smile as she looked around the room at her family. Her mother stood in front of the stove putting on the tea kettle. Her father and the kids had settled on the sofa in the family room. Jeff stood hovering beside her.

Her mother gave her a funny look. "Are you okay?"

Michelle started to nod, but stopped.

Kay stepped around the center island, reaching her hand out to her daughter. "What did the doctor say?"

Michelle could feel the tears welling in her eyes once more.

Kay grabbed her hands. "Is it bad?" she whispered.

Michelle lowered her head and Kay wrapped her in a tight embrace.

"Yes," Michelle choked out. Her mother held her close. It was all Michelle could do to not break down and cry in her mother's arms. She wiped the tears from her eyes and tried to put on a brave face before stepping away. She glanced over her shoulder at Jeff, just as he wiped a tear as well. She reached her hand out to him. He took it and squeezed gently.

"You ready for this?"

She shallowed hard. "I think so."

He touched his forehead to hers. "Together we face everything." He kissed the tip of her nose. "No matter how hard." Jeff took Michelle's arm and led her through the kitchen into the large family room.

She took a seat on the overstuffed sofa and patted the space on either side of her for the children while Jeff sat on the arm of the sofa.

Jack looked at his father with a puzzled look. "How come you aren't sitting in your chair?"

"I'm good right here."

"Then can I sit in it?" Jack started to get up.

Jeff put his hand on Jack's shoulder and said, "Stay beside your mother."

Frank and Kay sat on the loveseat nearby, while Shadow lay on the floor at Michelle's feet.

"What did the doctor say?" her mother asked.

"It's not good. I have a..." Michelle choked on the words "...b-brain tumor."

"No!" Beth flung her arms around her mother's neck. "It's not true, Mommy."

Michelle pulled her daughter onto her lap. "I'm afraid it is true."

Kay and Frank both gasped. "What are they going to do about it?" her father asked.

"Is it... *cancer*?" Her mother barely managed to voice the word.

"We won't know until they get the results of the biopsy." Michelle parted her hair and pointed to the tiny bandage. She grinned. "I actually do have a hole in my head." No one laughed.

"When will they operate?" Frank asked.

"It's inoperable."

"Radiation?" her father suggested.

Michelle shook her head. "It won't extend my life any longer."

"What does that mean?" her mother finally managed to whisper.

"All we can do is pray." Michelle looked at her children, their eyes full of fear. Her heart constricted with dread. How do you tell your children you are dying? She pulled them into her side. "The doctor th-thinks..." her voice broke, "...that I don't have much longer to live."

"NO!" Beth and Jack yelled at once. Beth threw her arms around her mother. "You can't die."

Jeff knelt down and hugged his family to him. The children sobbed into his chest.

Michelle fought back her own tears. If she started, she wasn't sure she could stop, and her family needed her strong, not falling apart. "We have to remember God is in control of everything. Even this." Michelle wiped the tears from her children's face. She kissed them on the top of their heads. She wanted to tell them everything would be okay. But would it?

Kay wiped her eyes, then stood up and said, "I'll make you some tea. The water is already hot." Michelle watched her mother take her time adding cream and sugar. Kay hung her head, no doubt giving herself a few moments to pull herself together. With a smile now on her face, she handed the cup to Michelle. She held onto it for an extra second before looking her daughter in the eyes and asking, "Did they..." she glanced down at her hands, "...say how long?"

Jeff shook his head. "Today, tomorrow, maybe three months. There's no telling."

"Today?" Beth's voice rose to hysterics. "You could die today?"

"Only God knows the answer to that." Michelle wiped her daughter's tears. Then she took a deep breath and smiled. "Nothing has really changed. I'm still here."

"But you're going to die," Jack sobbed.

Michelle hugged both children tightly. "All of us are going to die someday. We just don't know when." She kissed the tops of their heads again. "The only difference is the doctor has given me a visible timeline." She sighed. "No, we aren't happy about it, but we will not let it change who we are."

Jeff said, "We can pray for a miracle." He bowed his head and began, "Dear Heavenly Father, we have been blindsided with the news of Michelle's tumor. But we know You are not. We are overcome with grief. Please bring us comfort in our moment of trouble. And we ask in the name of Your son Jesus, for You to touch and heal Michelle. Thy will be done. Amen."

Together everyone said, "Amen." Michelle lifted her head. All eyes were on her—eyes filled with grief. Her heart crashed against her chest. Her children looked up at her as if begging her to fix this. She took a deep breath. Life was about the moments, not the length. And she vowed to give each one of them beautiful moments to treasure.

Michelle looked at her mother. "Something smells good."

"Grandma made your favorite—lasagna," Jack said.

"Yummy. Is it ready?" She patted her stomach. "I'm starving."

"It will be ready in a few minutes," Kay answered.

"Kids, go wash your hands, so you can help me set the table." Michelle started to get up, but Kay frowned. "No, you sit and relax."

Michelle ignored her and went into the dining room. Taking the china from the cabinet, she started setting the table. "Beth, you get the glasses. Jack, the silverware, please."

As they all sat, Jeff looked at the place settings. "The good china?"

"Yes." Michelle glanced around the table. "We are celebrating life."

A heaviness could be felt from every seat. After they said grace, Kay served the salad, lasagna and garlic bread. Michelle watched as everyone just pushed their food around. She looked at the mound on her own plate. The last thing she wanted to do was eat. Her stomach was tied up in knots and she wasn't even sure if she could swallow her food. She could feel the tears swelling. She closed her eyes tight and quietly prayed, "Give me the strength to be strong for them."

She put down her fork. "I don't think I have ever seen a bigger bunch of grumpy Gus's than are at this table." She glanced down at the dog. Even he looked sad. "Enough of this melancholy." She looked from one to the other, smiling at each of her loved ones. "Bad news does not ruin our day. It's time to put smiles on your faces and be happy."

"How can we be happy?" Jack asked.

"The same way we are every other day."

"Every other day you aren't d-d-dying," Beth's voice cracked.

"That isn't true." Michelle reached for her daughter's hand. "No one knows when they are going to be called home to Jesus. Every morning when we wake up, it's a gift from God. Something could happen to any of us to make this our last day on earth. The reality is that none of us knows when our life will end. So I want everyone to take a deep breath and hold it." They did. "Now I want you to release that breath, sending with it all the sadness you are feeling right now."

A loud rush of air filled the room.

She smiled. "Now, at the count of three, I want you all to say hallelujah. One, two, three."

At once, they weakly said, "Hallelujah."

Michelle shook her head. "Well, I know why none of us has been invited to join the choir, except for Beth." She smiled at her daughter. "Try it again. One, two, three."

This time they said it with more feeling.

"Now doesn't that make you feel better?"

They nodded half-heartedly.

"Whenever you are feeling sad, I want you to say hallelujah." She put her hand to her chest. "It's a word you can't say without feeling it in your heart." She picked up her fork and took a bite of lasagna, though even her taste buds felt numb. "Yum, this is delicious, Mom."

Kay mumbled her thanks.

"So, how was church yesterday?"

"You missed a good sermon," her father said.

Jack started to giggle. Frank tried to shush him.

"What's so funny?" Michelle eyed her son.

"Granddad told me to pull his finger in church."

"You did not!"

"He most certainly did." Kay rolled her eyes.

Jack and Beth started to laugh. "Mrs. Harris kept giving me the evil eye. So I pointed to Granddad and whispered, 'He did it'."

"Could Mrs. Harris smell it?" Jeff asked.

"The whole church could smell it." Kay now glared at her husband.

"That bad, huh?" Jeff asked, trying not to laugh.

"It was enough to gag a maggot." Jack's laughter was contagious and before they knew it everyone was laughing, talking and eating.

Michelle glanced at the clock on the microwave. "Jeff, it's almost five thirty. You and Jack need to get ready for practice."

"We're not going," Jeff said.

"Why not?"

"We're staying home with you." Jeff acted surprised that she would even ask.

"No, you're not." She gently touched the bandage on her head. "This will not stop us from living." Michelle stood, picked up her plate, and headed into the kitchen. "Go get ready."

Jack stormed out of the kitchen grumbling all the way upstairs.

"Michelle, what if—"

"It won't."

"How can you say that?"

"I don't even have a headache today. I'm fine. If something happens, Mom or Dad will call you." She laid a hand on his chest. "I'm fine."

He pulled her into his arms and whispered, "I'm so scared."

"I'm scared, too."

He gently caressed her back. "I can't be your hero and fix this."

She reached up and kissed him. "You will always be my hero. But this time we have to rely completely on God." She took a step back, gently pushing him away. "Now go get ready or you will be late for the first time ever."

Chapter 4

They had barely pulled out of the driveway when Jeff's cell phone rang. His heart slammed into his chest as Michelle's name displayed on the car's dash. He hit the answer button on the steering wheel. "Michelle." He couldn't keep the panic from his voice.

"I forgot to tell you... you need to pick up Timmy Smellie."

Jeff hadn't realized he'd stopped in the middle of the road until a car honked its horn behind him. "Okay."

A few minutes later, he pulled into the Smellie's driveway. The door to the house flew open and Timmy came running out, calling goodbye to whoever was inside. He scooted into the back seat beside Jack. "Hi, Jack. Hi, Mr. Jeff."

Jack mumbled hi and continued to stare out the window.

Jeff forced a smile at Timmy and said, "Buckle up."

At the ball field, Jeff pulled up beside Blake's truck. "Uncle Blake has the equipment today, so let's help him carry it to the field."

Timmy looked at Jack as the boy stormed over to the truck. Jeff came around in time to see Timmy hanging back. "Something the matter, Timmy?"

"Is Jack mad at me?"

Jeff put his hand on Timmy's shoulder. "No, he's just upset about some bad news we received today." They walked together to the back of Blake's truck.

"I'm surprised to see you here," his brother-in-law said.

Jack sighed, "Mom made us come."

"Of course she did," Annette said coming around the side of the truck. She pulled Jack into an embrace. "Your mother is all about living in the moment." She kissed the top of her nephew's head before letting him go. Then she laid her hand on Jeff's arm. "You doing okay?"

Jeff shrugged. "She said to tell you and Kimmy to come over instead of sitting here in the cold."

Annette grinned. "I was hoping she would be up for visitors."

Once they unloaded the equipment, Blake handed Annette his keys. "No need to come back for us. We can ride over with Jeff."

Annette reached up and gave her husband a swift kiss. "See you there."

Jeff and Blake had the boys run around the bases before dividing the team into two groups. Jeff took half for batting practice, while Blake took the others to play catch.

From the pitcher's mound, Jeff worked his way through the lineup. The last boy was Timmy. Snickers came from the bench as Timmy walked to the plate. Jeff tossed the first pitch and Timmy stood there, watching it fly by.

A boy named Charlie yelled, "Strike," and his friend Jason snickered.

Jeff pitched again. This time Timmy swung and missed.

"Strike two," Charlie yelled.

He and Jason nudged each other as the third ball flew by Timmy. One of them said loud enough for the others to hear, "Easy out."

"You'll get it next time," Jeff encouraged Timmy.

The other boys on the team echoed Jeff's encouragement except for Charlie and Jason.

Jeff pointed to Charlie and said, "You're up."

Charlie grabbed his bat and proudly walked to home plate. Over his shoulder, looking right at Timmy he said, "Watch and see how it's done."

Jeff smiled to himself. He had been an All-Star pitcher in college, and Charlie was about to get a lesson in humble pie.

He hurled a fastball and watched it fly by before the child could even swing.

"Strike one," Jeff yelled. He pitched again with the same result. "Strike two."

Charlie choked up on the bat, a move Jeff knew would be the boy's undoing.

This time Jeff pitched a curve ball. "Strike three."

Charlie flung his bat to the ground and turned to storm off.

"Pick it up." Jeff pointed at the bat. "We don't throw bats on this team. If you strike out, you take it like a man and walk off." Jeff turned to the bench and called, "Jason, your turn."

Jason took his stance at home plate, ready for the first pitch. He had the same results as his friend Charlie. Three strikes. Jason also started to throw his bat, but thought better of it, so instead he dragged the bat behind him.

Jeff called Jack to the pitcher's mound and handed him the ball. "Take over for me." Then he walked over to Charlie and Jason and said, "Grab your gloves and come with me."

"Why? What did we do?" Charlie asked.

Jeff motioned for them to follow. Inside he was steaming. In the two years he had been coaching, he had never had a bully on the team. This year would be no different. Today had not been the first time he had noticed Charlie and Jason picking on Timmy, but it would be the last. He took a deep breath and prayed his idea would work.

When they were a distance from the other boys Jeff turned toward them. "You two are new to the team, and so is Timmy." At the mention of Timmy's name the boys snickered. "I have been watching the two of you and you are both pretty good players. So I was wondering if you could help me with Timmy."

"What!" the boys said together.

Charlie started to turn away. "No one can help that loser." He nudged Jason in the ribs.

Jeff crossed his arms. "That kind of talk is not allowed on this team. No one is a loser."

"Have you seen him?" Charlie scoffed. "He can't do anything."

"He will get better. We just need to teach him. That's where you come in. I want the two of you to play catch with him. And help him learn how to throw."

"No way," Jason said. "We don't even like him."

"Why not?"

"Look at him," Charlie laughed. "He looks like a scarecrow in those big clothes. When he runs he almost trips himself. He can't hit, he can't catch or throw. He's hopeless." Charlie folded his arms across his chest. "I won't do it."

"And he smells," Jason added with a giggle.

"There was not one reason in there to not like someone," Jeff said. "And he doesn't smell."

"Even his name says he does." Both boys laughed.

"Enough," Jeff said firmly.

They abruptly stood at attention. "Well, no one at school likes him," Charlie muttered.

Jeff looked across the field at Timmy. "No one?"

"Well, Jack and Matt talk to him, but no one else."

Jeff felt a swell of pride that his son and nephew had befriended the new boy.

"You know it's really easy to follow the crowd. What's hard is to step up and be your own person." Jeff put his hands on the boys' shoulders. "You know I'm not asking you to like him. I'm asking you to help me teach him how to play."

"Don't know why you picked us." Charlie kicked at a blade of grass.

"I picked you, Charlie, because you have a long reach. I can put you in the outfield and with ease you can throw the ball clear across to home plate. No

41

problem. And Jason here, I can put him on first base and he can easily throw to anyone in the infield. But if I switched you two, you would both either overthrow or underthrow the ball. You have different strengths... which is why you make a good team. I need Timmy to see the difference in how to throw."

Charlie shrugged his shoulders. "Fine. But I'm not going to like him."

Jeff grinned. "All I'm asking is you give him some pointers." He called to Timmy, "Grab a glove and come over here." Timmy dashed over. "I want you to play catch with Charlie and Jason."

Timmy took a step back. "Why?"

Taking a ball from his pocket, Jeff handed it to Timmy. "Here's how this game is going to work. Timmy, you throw the ball to Charlie. If he misses, you get to ask him a question about his life. Then Charlie throws to Jason. If Jason misses, he has to answer a question. Then Jason throws to Timmy and he—You get the idea."

Timmy threw the ball and it didn't even go half the distance between him and Charlie. "Alright, ask Charlie a question."

"It's not my fault that I didn't catch it," Charlie objected. "He barely tossed it."

"Do you watch the Orioles play?" Jeff asked. Charlie nodded. "Do you ever see Adam Jones just standing in the outfield waiting for the ball to come to him? *No.* He hustles to the ball. If this was a game, Timmy would be on first base safe because you just stood there waiting for the ball."

Charlie folded his arms across his chest. "Whatever."

"Timmy, ask your question."

"What could I ask?"

"How about 'What does your father do'?"

Charlie shouted, "He's a lawyer."

Jeff handed the ball to Charlie and whispered, "Throw it over Jason's head."

"What?"

Jeff winked. "Do it."

Charlie grinned and lobbed his pitch way over Jason's head.

Jason jumped for the ball and missed. "Hey, that wasn't fair."

"Ask him the same question," Jeff prompted.

"What does your father do?"

"He's a cop."

Jason picked up the ball and hurled it to Timmy who unsurprisingly missed. "Okay, Timmy. Same question... what does your father do?"

Timmy hung his head. "He can't work."

Charlie and Jason snickered.

"Timmy," Jeff interrupted, "tell them what he did before the accident."

"He built and repaired bridges."

"What kind of bridges?" Charlie snickered. "Model ones?"

"No. Big ones."

"Tell them what happened."

Timmy puffed up his shoulders. "My Dad was doing repairs on the Chesapeake Bay Bridge when a speedboat ran into one of the beams." He moved his hands, imitating an explosion. "The bridge shook and my dad and another man fell off the platform."

Charlie and Jason's mouths fell open. "He fell off the bridge?" Charlie cautiously asked.

"No, they were wearing a harness." Timmy looked down at the ground. "But he hit the bridge and broke his back. Now he can't walk."

"Oh man, that's terrible," Charlie said.

Timmy then started to tell them how his dad used to climb to the top of any bridge no matter how high, and do whatever needed to be done. Charlie and Jason were impressed. Before long, the boys were playing catch and Timmy was actually catching a few.

Jeff glanced up the hill to where Michelle would normally be sitting. A wave of despair sucker-punched him. Was this the new normal? Life without Michelle? He knelt down on one knee, pretending to tie his shoe, and quickly wiped his face with the back of his hand. He added a quick prayer.

A loud cheer behind him brought Jeff back into the game. Charlie and Jason were jumping up and down. "You did it, Timmy." Timmy was grinning. Jason held the ball high in the air. "Mr. Jeff, Timmy threw the ball right into my glove."

"Great job!"

Blake walked up behind Jeff and put a hand on his back. "Don't know what you were thinking putting those three together, but it looks like it worked."

"I was thinking if they got to know Timmy and hear his story they would at the very least stop bullying him."

Jeff turned and called to the boys, "Time to join the others."

They returned to the field to practice catching and throwing. The time flew by and before they knew it, the parents who had left were back to get the boys.

They all loaded the equipment into the back of Jeff's truck. After the last parent departed, Jeff breathed a sigh of relief. This had been a long night and he was anxious to get home to Michelle.

Climbing into the back seat of the truck Jack said, "Timmy, you did really good tonight."

Timmy grinned from ear to ear.

"Yeah, Timmy," Jack's cousin Matt added, "before you know it you'll be just as good, if not better, than Charlie."

"I don't know. He's awful good."

"Keep practicing and you never know," Blake chimed in.

"Before my dad taught me to play, I couldn't even throw the ball a foot," Jack said.

"Really?"

"Yup." Jack grinned when he saw his father wink at him in the rearview mirror. Timmy didn't need to know he had been really little at the time. "My dad and uncle Blake are the best coaches ever."

The boys chatted nonstop until they pulled up to Timmy's house. The boy jumped out, ran across the yard, and into the house.

"That child has tons of energy," Jeff said backing out of the driveway.

All the anxiety he hadn't even realized he was holding onto lifted when he turned off the road and into his driveway. He had barely pulled the truck into the garage when the boys shot out of the truck.

"If we hurry, we can get to my Dad's chair."

"No playing with my chair," Jeff yelled after them.

Jack and Matt ran into the house, kicking their shoes off at the door. They both made a beeline through the kitchen into the family room, where Jack came to a screeching halt. His cousin ran into him, almost knocking him down.

"Granddad! You're in Dad's chair."

"Of course I am. It's the best chair in the house."

"But no one's allowed in it."

Frank started to get up but Jeff waved him back down. "I'm not ready to sit there yet." He winked at his father-in-law as he headed toward Michelle. "But when I am," he motioned with his thumb, "...you're out of there." He chuckled, then continued across the family room to where Michelle was sitting on the sofa. He leaned down and kissed her. "How are you feeling?"

"I'm good."

Kay pulled a Hoffman's ice cream cake from the freezer. "We sent Frank for dessert earlier. Anyone want some?"

The room shook with a loud, "Yes!"

Annette took plates from the cabinet, then placed them beside the cake. She then went to the bottom of the steps and called up to Beth and Kimmy. "Time for cake, girls."

The girls came running down squealing with delight.

It wasn't long before everyone left, and the kids were in bed. Jeff pulled Michelle down on his lap. "Hey, I'm sitting in your chair," she giggled.

"It's allowed if I'm with you."

Michelle laid her head on his chest. He held her tight. His heart ached with missing her already. He kissed the top of her head and realized he couldn't think like that. She was here in his arms right now and he would cherish this moment as he had all the others.

Chapter 5

Jeff's soft breathing normally would lure her to sleep, but not tonight. Michelle's mind was swirling with unanswered questions. If she fell asleep, would she wake up in the morning? She suppressed a sob. *No crying, no crying,* she kept repeating. To no avail, she felt the tears building again.

Softly, she slipped from the bed and tiptoed to the hallway. Gripping the banister, she cautiously went downstairs using the moonlight to guide her through the kitchen and out onto the patio. Her bare feet touched the cold stone, taking her breath away. For a brief moment, she thought about going back inside. Instead her feet propelled her up the stone path to the heart full of tulips where she collapsed to the ground.

Michelle covered her face with her hands. Tears streamed down her cheeks. *Why me, God? Did I do something wrong?* Question after question flowed with her tears. *Will I see my children's faces one more time? Or feel the joy of my husband's arms? I am weak. I can't handle this. Please,* she sobbed into her hands, *please take this burden from me.*

She felt the warmth of her husband's arm go around her as he knelt beside her. "You shouldn't be sitting on this cold ground." He wrapped her in an embrace and guided her to her feet, before lifting her into his arms. She buried her face in his chest while he carried her to the garden bench, and sat with her on his lap.

Her voice broke, "I don't want to d-die."

Jeff held her tight.

"I will never see our kids' first dates, them graduate from school, or get married." Her sob broke in half. "I will never be a grandmother." She touched his face. "I won't grow old with you." Jeff's tears now mingled with hers.

Suddenly the sky opened up and rain came pouring down. Jeff jumped to his feet and started running toward the house with her still in his arms.

Michelle flung back her head and began to laugh. "Stop," she commanded. "Put me down." The moment her feet touched the wet ground Michelle started to twirl around, her hands in the air, her face lifted to the sky. The rain mingled with her tears. She couldn't stop laughing. "Looks like God poured a bucket of water on my pity party." She grabbed Jeff's hand and started to dance with him.

Happiness welled in her as her husband's arms held her tight. This was what life was all about, wonderful moments of pure joy. Then the shower stopped as quickly as it had started. She stood on her tiptoes and kissed Jeff, then glanced up at the stars that were starting to peek out again. "Thank you, God."

Jeff laughed, "Only you would thank God for nearly drowning us."

"Don't you get it? God washed my fears away, and replaced them with this moment of love. This is what life is all about—dancing in the rain with the man I love."

He picked her up and twirled her. "Yes, I get it. He gave me this moment to treasure forever."

Jeff carried her into the house. After he put her down on the tile floor, he turned to close the French doors. A puddle of water was already at their feet. "Good thing someone was smart, and used ceramic wood tiles instead of real hardwood."

Michelle patted his chest. "That's why I married you. You are so smart."

"Here I thought you married me for my good looks and charm."

"That too." She looked at the trail of water they were leaving. "On second thought, if someone was so smart we would have come in the mud room and not the family room."

Jeff's mouth flew open, and he chuckled. "Good thing I still have the charm."

"Good thing." She winked at him as she grabbed his hand and pulled him into the laundry room. She handed him a bath towel from the stack right inside the door.

Michelle flipped her head over and wrapped a towel around her long hair. She rubbed it between her hands to get the excess water out.

"Your hair is getting curlier by the minute," he said.

She rolled her eyes. "It loves to be wet."

Jeff pulled the towel from her hair. "I love it wet, too."

She pulled another towel off the stack and swatted him with it.

He kissed her forehead. "We need to get out of these wet clothes," he said pulling his shorts off.

Michelle let her nightgown fall to the floor and stepped out of it. She wrapped the dry towel around herself and continued to dry off. Jeff grabbed her towel with both hands and pulled her to him. Eagerly wrapping her arms around his neck, she pulled his lips to hers. The passion of their love for each other carried the kiss into a heated embrace.

Once more Jeff carried her, this time upstairs where he locked the bedroom door.

Chapter 6

Michelle slowly awoke. Before she opened her eyes, she silently prayed, *Thank you.* She glanced at the clock—five thirty. *Oh no!* She tossed the covers off and started to jump up. They had overslept. Her feet barely touched the floor when she remembered today was the start of a new way of living. She lay back down and cuddled up against Jeff's back. Since she would be unable to drive, Jeff would be waiting to go to work until after he dropped the kids off at the bus stop. Perks of being the boss. She debated whether to get up or snuggle under the covers a little longer.

God had granted her another day. She would not waste it sleeping. She quietly crawled out of bed, grabbed clothes from the dresser, and tiptoed to the bathroom, thanking God with each step for the gift of this day. She didn't turn the light on until she closed the door behind her.

Michelle dressed, brushed her teeth and hair, and slipped out of the room. Before heading down the stairs, she peeped in on the kids. Shadow lay on the floor beside Jack's bed. He raised his head to look at her then dropped it back down.

Downstairs, she put the water on for some tea and made sure the coffee started to brew for Jeff. Then she grabbed her Bible and headed into the sunroom. Opening the patio door, she debated whether to go outside or not. A blast of cold air greeted her.

She stepped outside and put her arms in the air. The cold made her feel alive. She dropped to her knees, hugging her Bible to her chest. For a few minutes, she knelt there listening to the birds sing as they too started their day. She embraced the quiet communion with God until the teapot whistled and she went inside.

Today might be the last time she would put the tea bag into her tulip cup. She traced the outline of the ruffled rim, following the shape of the tulip, remembering the day Jeff had brought the set home. He had been on his way to a job, and out of the corner of his eye noticed it in a store window. He made a U-turn and spent way more than they could afford at the time. Love in a tea cup. She smiled. How had she gotten so lucky to have been given this awe-inspiring love that had grown with each passing day?

One of the many blessings God had given her. She carried her beverage to the sunroom. Sitting down on the sofa, she pulled the prayer list from her Bible and read the names on the list. She smiled when she got to Dr. Carson's name. Jennifer had asked Michelle to pray for his salvation... now Michelle had another reason to pray for him—God's guidance in her healing. She bowed her head and prayed. With a song in her heart, she opened her Bible and started to read.

When the sun peeked over the hill, a tiny ray of light led a path to her tulips, their garden of blessings. Overwhelmed at the visual reminder of how blessed she was, her heart swelled.

Today was a good day. Nothing could take that away from her. She headed into the kitchen humming as she mixed up waffle batter. For a moment, sadness filled her... would this be the last time she made waffles?

No! She would not allow that thought to ruin her day. A different idea popped into her head. She should make extra and freeze them for when she was gone. It filled her heart with joy that she would still be able to give her family this gift. She smiled to herself and mixed a triple batch.

She was just pulling the waffle maker out when Jeff came into the kitchen and headed right over to her. With a kiss he said, "Good morning."

"Yes, it is."

He eyed the waffle maker. "Waffles on a work day?"

"I woke up early, so yes." She handed him his coffee before pouring the batter.

"Are we having company this morning?"

"No, why?"

"There's enough in that bowl to feed an army."

She laughed. "I can always freeze whatever we don't eat." She shooed him out of the way. "The Bible is on the table in the sunroom."

He took a sip of the coffee. "You coming?"

She shook her head. "I already had my quiet time." He looked surprised. "I think that's why God woke me so early. He needed me to be still with Him this morning."

Jeff nodded. "The kids will be up soon, so I better get mine in." He had barely been gone a few minutes when he ran back in with the Bible in hand. "Listen to this. *Psalm 118:17* says, *I will not die but live, and will proclaim what the LORD has done."* He repeated it. "Michelle, we need to claim this verse."

Michelle whispered, "*I will not die but live, and will proclaim what the LORD has done.*" She placed her hand on her heart. "Thy will be done." She finished making the last waffle. "I'm going to go wake the kids."

She first went into Beth's room. "Time to wake up, sleepyhead."

Beth's eyes flew open and she bolted up. "Mommy, you're alive."

Michelle sat on the edge of the bed. "And so are you, so time to get up for school."

"Can't I stay home with you?"

"No staying home."

"But what if you die, and no one is with you?"

Michelle hugged Beth tight. "Oh, baby, I don't want you to worry about me dying."

Beth wiped a tear. "I don't want you to die."

Michelle brushed Beth's curly blonde hair from her face. "Everyone dies. We don't know when, we just know it is going to happen. With me, we only know it will be soon, but we still don't know when. Only God knows that. We can't focus on the dying. God wants..." Michelle smiled, "...and I want... us to enjoy each day we have left together. I don't want you to worry or be sad."

"How can I not be sad?"

"This is how." Michelle started to tickle Beth. The child's laughter drew Jack into the room, and he dove on the bed beside them. Michelle reached for him and started to tickle him, too.

"Hey, what's all the racket?" Jeff asked. "How dare you have a tickle party and not invite me?" He jumped into the middle of the bed.

"Stop," Michelle begged between laughs. "I'm going to pee myself."

Beth untangled herself from the pile. "Me too." She made a mad dash to the bathroom. Wiping tears of laughter from her face, Michelle pulled herself off the bed. "That was a fun way to start the day." She kissed Jeff and Jack on the cheek and said, "Now let's go eat."

Jack ran down the stairs, skidding to a stop at the sight of breakfast. "Beth, we're having waffles. Hurry up!" he shouted.

"Today is a good day." Michelle lifted her orange juice glass in a toast. The others joined her.

After the plates were cleaned away, Michelle followed the kids upstairs to get dressed. When she started to put on dress clothes for work, Jeff asked, "What are you doing?"

"Getting ready for work, what else?"

"You can't go to work."

"Why not?"

"You need to rest."

"I'm not an invalid."

"You need to take it easy."

Michelle put her hands on her hips. "You want me to claim that verse and yet you don't want me to act like it's true. What would God think of that?" She turned back to the mirror and continued to fix her hair. "Until I can't, I will keep doing as I always have. Faith, Jeff, is all we can do." She brushed the top of her hair back, pinning it with a jeweled barrette.

"But I'll be at the Columbia worksite most of the day. What if something happens?"

"If something happens, it won't really matter if you are here in Maryland or halfway to the moon. It's going to happen anyway."

"I meant, how will you get back home if you get a bad headache?"

"It's not that far. I could walk."

"No way."

"I do have an assistant, you know. She can drive me home... just like she'll be driving me to the jobs and the nursery."

"Is Nicole even old enough to drive?"

Michelle giggled. "She's in college."

"Well, she looks like a baby."

Michelle patted his arm. "She can drive."

"Have you seen her driving record?"

This time Michelle snorted. "Since when have you turned into a mother hen?" She slipped on her shoes and left the bedroom. "I'm going to get the kids moving."

Jeff drove them down the mile-long driveway and waited for the bus. Their construction and landscape company was just at the end of their road. "You sure this is a good idea?" he asked.

"Jeff, yes."

The minute he opened the office door and Michelle walked in, her sister-in-law, Debbie, flew from her seat and rushed to Michelle. She wrapped her in a tight hug. "What are you doing here?" Others from the office gathered around.

"I work here."

"But..."

"Today is a good day."

"You're feeling alright?"

"Yes, the medicine they gave me for the headaches is actually working." Michelle looked around at the group of employees. She smiled. "I'm fine, and nothing has changed. It's work as usual."

The phone started to ring so Debbie hurried to answer it. Jeff nodded at the others. "Time to get back to work," he said. He followed Michelle into her office. "Seems like they all know."

"Well, once you told your family, you knew Debbie would tell everyone."

He nodded. "Should we call a meeting?"

"Good idea. We can call a meeting in ten minutes and another one for the guys in the field when they get back this afternoon. Or just wait and do it all at once."

"I think for those that are here it would be better to do it now."

"I agree."

Jeff nodded. "I'll tell Debbie to let everyone know."

When everyone had gathered in the conference room, Michelle said, "As you all have heard, I have a brain tumor." There was a collected gasp. "I want you all to know, that for now it is business as always. Nothing has changed. The only restriction the doctor gave me concerning work is that I can't drive." She looked at Nicole and added, "So I will be depending on you for that."

Nicole nodded.

"I'll continue to design the landscape for houses you build and remodel, and my crew will implement those plans as usual—making the outside as beautiful as the work you all do on the inside." She looked around the room. The sad faces of the crew brought tears to her eyes. "Life is a gift and today has been granted for each of us. Let us all make it the best day yet."

Jeff put his arm around her, pulling her to his side. He kissed the top of her head.

Michelle smiled up at him. "What's on the agenda for today?"

They left the conference room hand in hand. Jeff walked with Michelle to her office where he perched on the edge of her desk. "Are you sure this is a good idea?"

Sighing, Michelle turned on her computer. "Yes." She pointed to the door. "You have a crew of guys waiting for you."

He leaned across the desk to give her a kiss. "I love you."

"Love you, too. Now get to work."

"Please take it easy."

"I will." She pulled out her day planner and pretended to write in it. "Easy day."

"I'm serious."

"I thought you were Jeff."

He laughed and walked out the door.

A few minutes later, Nicole came in with a cup of tea. "Thank you, Nicole." Michelle pointed to the chair in front of her desk. "Let's talk. For now, like I said to the others, it's business as usual. I will be needing you to drive me around, and possibly take the lead on more jobs."

Nicole kept her head down, but Michelle could see the young woman's streaked face. She got up and walked around the desk, kneeling in front of Nicole and grasping her hands. "I want you to embrace whatever life brings us today. The sun is shining, the birds are singing, and flowers are starting to bloom. Today is an awesome day." She stood to retrieve her day planner from her desk. "Yesterday, I had planned to go to the house in Sykesville to take some pictures and measurements." She glanced at her watch. "What time is your class today?"

"One o'clock, so I have to leave here by noon."

Michelle glanced at the time on her cell phone. "It's almost ten now. We have just enough time to get some pictures. If we run short, I can always use Google Earth to get rough estimates of the space later." Michelle reached into her purse for the keys to her company car, then handed them to Nicole. "You get to drive." Then she grabbed her camera and a drawing pad from the side table.

"We probably ought to wear boots," Nicole said. "It rained on Sunday and I'm sure the ground is still muddy."

"Good idea." Michelle slipped off her flats and stepped into her boots by the office door. It took them less than fifteen minutes to get to the job site.

Michelle looked at the once green lawn that now was filled with huge ruts. "Boy, did they do a number on this yard."

"I drive by here every day on my way to school and thought the same thing."

Michelle stepped out of the car right into a mud puddle. "First thing we do is get this driveway leveled off so the water doesn't sit in the middle like this."

Nicole wrote that down while Michelle tried to sidestep the puddles. It didn't take them long to snap pictures of the house and yard from all sides. "It's really too muddy to get measurements right now. We can do that another day." Michelle paused before turning to the backyard. "Let's see how the back looks."

Nicole followed her with the measuring wheel. "Not as messy back here."

"Eek!" Michelle's feet slipped out from beneath her. The impact of her head hitting the ground sent a shock wave through her. Unable to move, she waited for the flash of pain that would end her life. She closed her eyes, trying to still the rush of blood flowing to her head. *Please God, not today.*

Nicole dropped to her knees and grabbed Michelle's hands. "Are you okay? What can I do? Should I call Jeff? 911?" Questions spilled from her one on top of another.

Those wide eyes and pale face pushed Michelle out of her stupor. "I'm okay." She reached up, touching Nicole's face. "Just help me up."

"Are you sure?"

"Yes." She slowly sat up, but then remained still for a moment. Amazed there was no headache, she gingerly touched her head.

"Does it hurt?"

"No." Michelle giggled. "Guess my head is harder than I thought."

Back at the office, Michelle put her hand on the back door knob. She glanced at Nicole's muddy clothes. "You might as well leave now, that way you can go change before class."

Nicole glanced down at her knees. "Do you want me to take you home so you can get clean clothes, too?"

"No, I learned a long time ago to keep a change of clothes here."

"Okay, I'll see you tomorrow."

Michelle had barely sat down at her desk when her sister flew into the office.

"Why are you at work?" Annette asked accusingly.

"Why wouldn't I be?"

"You need to be home resting," Annette said.

Michelle sighed. "I really wish everyone would stop acting like I'm an invalid."

"The doctor said—"

"I know what the doctor said. I also know that God is in control of my life. I can do nothing to change the outcome. What I can do is control how my days on earth, no matter how short they may be, will be spent. I, for one, am going to make every day count for something. I will not focus on the dying, but on the living."

Annette hugged her. "What are we going to do?"

"We are going to fill each day with love and wonderful memories. I'm hungry," she said. "Let's go get some lunch and make a good memory for you to cherish later."

Over sandwiches Annette said, "I just don't understand why you think you need to be at work."

"It's not work to me." Michelle took a bite of her salad. "I love what I do. It makes me feel like I'm playing a small role in beautifying the earth, one house at a time."

"I never did understand your fixation with flowers and trees."

Michelle grinned. "And lily ponds."

"Oh yes, let's not forget the ponds." Annette started to snicker. "Remember your first attempt at making one?"

Michelle almost choked on her food trying not to laugh. "Grandmother was so mad that I dug up her peonies."

"But Granddad thought it was funny."

"He understood that was the best place for a lily pond. And I did transplant the peonies to a better place."

"Once they came up again, grandmother finally forgave you."

"And so a career was born."

"What were you, six?"

Michelle nodded. "And now I put a lily pond or some kind of water feature in every design. But I learned my lesson with that first one. Now I have someone else do all the work."

"Um… if I recall, you had Granddad do most of the work even back then." They both laughed.

"You know what would be fun?"

Annette eyed her with suspicion.

"Let me design a lily pond in your backyard."

"Now?"

"Yes."

Michelle grabbed her purse and stood. Annette stared at her. Michelle reached for her hand, pulling her sister up from the seat. "You know, I've always wanted to do this for you. Let me do it now."

They both felt the unspoken words, *before I can't.*

"Okay," Annette squeezed her hand, "promise me there will be no digging."

Michelle hugged her. "I promise today will just be the planning."

An hour later, Annette dropped Michelle back off at work. Looking at the drawing in her hand she said, "This is going to be breathtaking," and leaned over to kiss Annette's cheek. "Thank you for making today awesome. Love you." She entered the office humming.

Debbie glanced up as soon as the office door opened. "How are you feeling?" She rushed to Michelle's side.

"I'm doing good." Michelle patted Debbie's arm. "Really, I am."

"Can I take you home?"

"No. I have some work to do." Michelle sat at her desk and pulled the disk out of her camera to put it into the computer.

"Can I get you some tea?" Debbie offered.

Michelle started to say no, but the look of concern on Debbie's face reminded her she was not the only one the tumor affected. Michelle smiled. "Yes, that would be great." She picked up the mug from her desk. Its verse made her smile. "*When you go through deep waters, I will be with you. Isaiah 43:2.*" Her heart filled with hope. Jeff had bought her that mug after they had gone fishing on the bay and a storm came out of nowhere. They had almost been washed overboard. If not for Jeff's strength—and God's help—they would have. Now they were washed overboard in a different storm, but God was still with them.

She handed the mug to Debbie. "Read what's on it."

"Wow, I love it."

"Me too."

Michelle printed out the job site pictures she had taken.

Debbie brought them in from the printer as she walked by and placed both the tea and photos on Michelle's desk. "Anything else I can help you with?"

"No. I'm just going to get everything ready so the kids can help me make a model of the Sykesville house and land. They love doing that."

"So do you."

"Yes… I do." Michelle took a sip from her mug. "Thanks for the tea. It's perfect."

Debbie backed out of the office. "If you need me, call."

Chapter 7

Days turned into weeks. Michelle barely had a headache. The threat of dying hovered in the background like an unwanted guest. She cheerfully chatted to Nicole as they wandered the aisle of the nursery.

"Look at this one," Michelle said, leaning down to smell the pink and white peony. "It's not only beautiful, but they're on sale." She gently touched the outer pink petals. "I love how the white center is ruffled. It's almost like getting two flowers in one." She placed the plant on the cart. "I think we should get two of each kind." She pointed to a dark pink bush. "Those would look great next to the lighter pinks and the whites."

When she stooped to pick up the next plant, a bolt of stabbing pain slashed through her brain. She grabbed her head, putting pressure on it, hoping to ease the agony. Within minutes, she could barely see out of her right eye.

She grabbed Nicole's arm. "I need to sit down," she said and turned to leave. "I'll wait in the car while you finish up."

"I'll walk you to the car." Nicole took her by the arm.

Once Michelle was settled, Nicole hurried back to get their purchases. Michelle leaned the seat back, closed her eyes, and prayed she wouldn't get sick. It was all she could do on the ride home not to scream when every bump in the road caused hot searing pain to pierce her head. Never was she so grateful to pull up to her front door.

"Are you going to be alright by yourself?" Nicole asked, as she helped Michelle from the car.

"Yes. I just need to lay down for a little bit."

"Should I call Jeff?"

"No. It's just a migraine." She unlocked the front door. "I've had them like this before. I just need to go to sleep."

"You need me to help you upstairs?"

"No." She stepped through the doorway. "You need to get those flowers back to the shop and out of the hot car." She watched Nicole head off before she closed the door. She leaned against it for a moment. Shadow came running and Michelle patted the dog's head.

When she started toward the stairs, Shadow blocked her way. "Come on, boy, I can't play right now. I need to lay down." The dog refused to move. Tiny balls of light danced across her vison. "Please move."

Shadow nudged her hand until she knelt and said, "Okay, I will pet you for a minute then you have to let..."

Michelle tried to open her eyes. Where was she? What was heavy on her chest? Slowly she forced her eyes open. Confusion washed over her. Why was she on the floor? How did she get home? And why was Shadow laying on her?

She tried to sit up, but was too weak. She closed her eyes again and fell back to sleep. When she opened them some time later, she was finally able to sit up. "Why am I on the floor?" she asked the dog.

Grabbing hold of the stair railing, Michelle managed to pull herself up. Her legs buckled under her. How was she going to make it up the stairs? She needed to lay down. Using the wall for support, she made it into the main floor guest room and crawled onto the bed.

Even before he had hung up from Nicole's call, Jeff took off running toward his truck. Every few minutes he would redial Michelle's number. Each unanswered call stabbed him in the heart. It was the longest thirty minutes of his life. Jumping from the truck, he dashed into the house. Seeing Michelle's purse laying open on the floor nearly choked the breath from him. "Michelle!" he yelled.

Shadow came to the door of the guest bedroom.

"What are you doing in there, boy?" Jeff walked to the door to shut it, but saw Michelle lying across the bed. One look at her pale face and his heart crashed into his chest. He ran across the room. "Michelle, are you alright?"

Jeff brushed hair from her face and felt her breath on his skin. He bowed his head. *Thank you, Jesus. She's still alive.*

Michelle barely opened her eyes.

"What can I do for you?" he offered.

"Water," she whispered.

"Let me get you under the covers first." Jeff removed her shoes, then pulled the pale green comforter over her. He hurried to the kitchen for some water. On his return, he lifted her head and placed the glass to her mouth.

Michelle barely took a sip before closing her eyes again.

Shadow looked at Michelle and whimpered, laying his head on the edge of the bed and watching her sleep.

Jeff patted the dog. "What happened, boy?" Jeff quietly backed out of the room. He stood slightly away from the door, where he could still see his wife. Pulling his phone from the clip, he called Nicole. "Would you mind bringing the kids home when they get off the bus? I'm not going to be able to leave Michelle."

"What happened?" she gasped.

"I don't know, but she's really out of it."

"I knew something wasn't right. She seemed like she was in a daze."

Michelle moaned.

"I need to get back to her," Jeff said, then pushed the end button on his phone. "Sweetheart, are you hurt?"

She stared at him with blank eyes for a minute before drifting back to sleep. Jeff sat on the overstuffed chair in the corner of the room. *Please God, don't let this be the end. I beg you, please.*

Shadow lifted his head and his ears perked up just before the front door flew open with a bang. Jeff hurried into the hallway, put a finger to his lips, and whispered, "Quiet."

The kids dropped their bookbags on the floor by the front door. Suddenly, Beth looked at her Dad. Fear flashed in her eyes and she rushed to her father's side, glancing into the room to see her mother on the bed. "Is she..." Beth's voice broke.

Jeff quickly wrapped his arms around them. "She's just sleeping."

When Michelle opened her eyes, darkness was all around. Confusion washed over her. There was a wall where there should be a window. Whose bed was this? Jeff's arm was around her. How did they get here, and where was *here*? She rolled over.

Jeff immediately whispered, "Are you okay?"

"Where are we?"

"The guest room."

"Why?"

"Don't you remember coming in here?"

"No." She sat up, swinging her legs off the bed. Her foot touched the top of Shadow's head. "Boy, what are you doing in here?"

"He hasn't left your side since before I came home."

"But he always sleeps with Jack."

"We couldn't get him to move, not even to eat. So we fed him in here."

Michelle started to stand.

"Where are you going?" Jeff held her by the arm.

"To the bathroom."

"I'll help you." He started to get up as well.

"You are not helping me to the bathroom. Are you crazy?" She shook her head. "Go back to sleep."

She could feel Jeff's eyes on her as she walked to the adjoining bathroom. The light blinded her, so she immediately turned it off. When she soon crawled back into bed, Shadow left the room. They could hear him going upstairs.

Jeff chuckled. "The crisis must be over. Shadow left you for Jack."

"What crisis?"

"Don't you remember anything?"

"No. Just being at the office and asking Nicole to drive us to the nursery."

"You don't remember coming home?"

"No."

"Did you have another seizure?"

"I don't know."

Her husband wrapped his arm around her, pulling her close.

She laid her head on his chest. "I just know I am really tired." She fell asleep wondering why she couldn't remember anything after that morning.

Chapter 8

Jeff was on his way to check out a job when he noticed an older couple—both with walkers—struggling to carry a ladder across their yard. One end of the ladder was resting on the old woman's walker and the other end was on the old man's. The man would tell the woman when to take a step. It was like watching a cartoon, the way they waddled across the yard. Jeff laughed out loud watching them.

It wasn't until he passed their driveway that it fully registered what he was seeing. What were they doing?

He made a U-turn and drove back. They stopped struggling for a moment and looked at him as he got out of his truck. "You need some help?" he called.

The woman said in relief, "Oh, yes."

"Here, let me get this for you." Jeff lifted the ladder before he realized the old man was caught inside the rungs. He tried not to laugh. "How did you get in there?"

The man grinned. "Like this." He lowered his end of the ladder to the ground and stepped out.

"Where are you going with it?"

"To clean the rainspouts," the man said.

"What!"

"I told him it wasn't a good idea for him to climb a ladder when he can barely walk, but he wouldn't listen." The woman put her hands on her hips. "So there was no way he was going to do this alone."

"Why didn't you call someone to help you?"

"Kids and grandkids live too far away."

Jeff put the ladder up against the old farm house and started to climb. The old man raised his hand. "Hoooo. I can do it."

"I don't think so."

"I can't afford to pay you."

"Not asking you to." Jeff climbed the ladder and stepped onto the roof.

"Shouldn't you stay on the ladder?" the woman asked.

"It's easier this way." On hands and knees Jeff crawled along the roof line, pulling stuff out of the gutters. When he got to the end, he stood up and walked to the top of the roof and disappeared down the other side.

"Hey Mister, you okay up there?" the man yelled as he and his wife tried to hurry to the other side of the house.

Jeff yelled back, "Yup." It wasn't long before he came around the back of the house. "All done."

"How'd you get down?"

"Jumped."

"You could have gotten hurt!" the woman gasped.

Jeff laughed and said, "You sound like my mother." He patted the old lady's hand. "I've been jumping off of roofs since I was a kid. Nothing to worry about."

There was a large branch laying on the ground. He went to step over it when he noticed a broken window on the main floor with a cardboard covering. "I can fix that for you."

"Mister, I can't pay you."

Jeff held out his hand. "Jeff Stevens."

The man took his hand and said, "I'm Clarence, and this is Edith."

"Nice to meet you."

Jeff went to the truck and found his tape measure before returning to the side of the house.

"We can't pay you," the old man repeated.

"You don't have to." Jeff looked at the couple and smiled. "I'll be back in a few hours to fix that window, and I'll have my crew either this afternoon or tomorrow trim the dead branches out of that tree before it breaks another window."

Edith said, "Why don't you come in and wash your hands and have a piece of coconut cake and coffee before you leave?"

"Edith makes the best coconut cake in town," Clarence said.

"How can I pass that up?" Inside, Jeff went to the kitchen sink and turned on the hot water tap. After thirty seconds, it kept running cold. "You having trouble with your hot water?"

"Don't know what's wrong with it," the man said, dropping his gaze. "Haven't been able to get down to the basement to see what the problem is."

Jeff turned off the water. "Let me take a look."

Clarence walked Jeff to the basement stairs. "I used to fix everything around here. Now I'm not much good for anything."

"Don't you go talking like that," Edith said. "You are good for a lot of things." She hugged her husband. "The most important one is loving me."

Clarence kissed his wife on the lips. "Married going on sixty-five years and the sparks are still there." He winked at Jeff.

"If I help you down the stairs, do you think you can make it?"

Clarence grinned. "I sure can." Jeff slowly helped Clarence one stair at a time. Once at the bottom, Jeff ran back up to retrieve the walker.

Clarence showed him where the hot water heater was and Jeff checked it out.

"Looks like the heating element has gone bad." Jeff took a picture of the water heater with his cell phone. "I'll get this fixed today for you."

"We—"

Jeff raised his hand to stop Clarence. "My wife and I take ten percent off the top of our business profits and put it in an account for situations just like this."

"You and your wife must be special people."

"My wife sure is."

Back upstairs, Edith had the coffee and cake waiting. Jeff took one bite and said, "Wow, you weren't lying when you said it's the best."

Jeff left them promising to be back in a few hours. After he'd climbed into his truck, he sat staring at the house. *Sixty-five years and still in love.*

His own heart filled with love, knowing he and Michelle would be like that in another fifty-five years. Then his heart slammed into his chest. He couldn't breathe. They didn't have years. He lay his head on the steering wheel and let the tears come. Tears for years stolen.

After a few minutes, he lifted his head and looked toward the sky. "I don't think I can handle this, God. Please don't take her from me."

He heard Michelle's voice saying *hallelujah* in his mind.

"Hallelujah," he whispered, then wiped his face with the back of his hand and backed out of the driveway.

Chapter 9

"I made tacos for dinner tonight," Michelle said when Jeff walked in the door.

He leaned down and kissed her. "Smells good."

"I'll get them on the table in a few minutes." She glanced at the clock. "Beth, can you pour everyone some peach iced tea?"

Jack was playing with Shadow. "Jack, get to the table," Jeff called. "We don't have a lot of time before we need to leave for your game."

Jack skidded to his seat. "We have a good team this year, don't we, Dad?"

"We sure do."

Pushing his shoulders back Jack said, "We're even good enough to win the playoffs."

"No sense counting your chickens before they hatch."

"Huh?"

"You can't win something you haven't made yet," Jeff explained.

Between bites, Jack replied, "We will. I just know it."

At the field before the game, Jeff gave a glance to the top of the hill where Michelle sat with Annette.

Shadow had run off to the playground with Beth and Kimmy. Jeff smiled at his wife. Life was good. Michelle hadn't missed a game, and his team had only lost one so far.

He turned back to the field. Timmy was the first to bat. Everyone cheered when the new boy's bat made contact with the ball and he ended up on second base. Charlie was next, and he hit the ball hard enough to bring Timmy home. The other boys lined up in the dugout, taking turns slapping Timmy on the back.

Never had Jeff felt such a sense of pride. After a rough start, the boys had taken Timmy under their wings and taught him better than Jeff or Blake ever could have. He said a quick thank you to God.

Baseball was a large part of their lives. Three times a week they were at the field and before each game, Jeff would glance up the hill at Michelle. Was it really only a month and a half since his world had come crashing down? Seeing her now laughing at something one of the other mothers had said, you would never know the death sentence she carried.

Jeff shook his head. No, God was answering their prayers. Yes, life was good.

"Honey, I'm home." His words fell on an empty kitchen. Jeff placed his lunch box on the counter and lifted the lid of the pot on the stove. His stomach growled at the aroma of meat sauce that wafted up.

Shadow's bark drifted in from the patio. Jeff put the lid back on and headed out to join his family.

Jeff's heart swelled with joy as he watched his family enjoying the spring weather. Jack and Shadow were running around the yard. Michelle and Beth had their heads together, giggling as Michelle wrote in a notebook.

"What are you two doing?" Jeff asked.

Michelle jerked her head up. "Wow, I didn't realize it was that late." She closed her notebook. "Beth and I were planning the girl's weekend."

"Why?"

"Because it's going to be here."

"I thought it was Debbie's turn," he said.

"It was supposed to be, but I wanted to host it."

Jeff kneeled down beside his wife, then lifted her face with his finger so he was looking her in the eyes. "I don't think that's a good idea."

"Why not?"

Jeff frowned. "You have to ask?"

Michelle touched her lips to his. "Dinner will be ready in about ten minutes." Before heading into the kitchen, she called to Jack, "Time to come in."

"Michelle, I don't think it should be here," Jeff said and followed her into the house.

She turned with her hands on her hips. "There is no reason why it can't be here."

"It's not your turn."

"It is now." She glanced at Beth and smiled. "We're planning the best weekend ever."

Beth poked Jack in the arm. "Our time will be so much better than your boy's weekend."

"I don't think so." Jack pretended to cast his fishing rod. "A weekend of fishing and sleeping under the stars... nothing could be better than that."

"We're going to bake cookies and have manicures, then watch movies and swim."

"Oooh," Jack flipped his hand. "My nails are wet." He laughed. "Doesn't sound fun to me."

"But smelly fish does?" The children continued arguing.

"Go wash your hands and set the table," Michelle said. "You can finish this discussion later."

Jeff carried the pot of pasta to the sink and poured it into the strainer. "We'll continue this discussion later, too."

"Nothing to discuss." Michelle mixed the salad and handed it to Beth to place on the table. "It will be here." She patted her daughter's hand. "And it will be the best girl's weekend ever."

"No, it won't." Jeff slammed the pot into the sink. The kids stared wide eyed at him.

Michelle spun around. "What is your problem?"

"I don't want—"

"It's not about what you want." She waved her hand around the room. "It's about what is best for the family." She put her hands on his hips. "And what is best for the family is for you to pull yourself together." She touched his arm. "Life is a gift and I—we—will make the most of each and every day."

Jeff closed his eyes. "What if it's too much for you?"

"It won't be." She went to the refrigerator and read the verse posted there. "*I will not die but live, and will proclaim what the LORD has done.* Why did you print this out?"

"To remind us never to give up hope."

"Then why are you?"

Jeff pulled Michelle into his arms. "You're right." He looked at the kids. "I'm sorry."

Jack shouted, "Hallelujah!"

Michelle giggled. Jeff broke into a grin and spun Michelle around singing, "Hallelujah." Within moments, they were dancing around the kitchen, laughing.

Chapter 10

"Man, I forgot to get the crew over here this week to cut Clarence and Edith's grass," Jeff said as they drove by the older folks' house on their way to the ballfield.

"Didn't you say their daughter was coming tomorrow for Mother's Day?" Michelle asked, glancing at the overgrown yard.

"Yes." Jeff shook his head. "Now I feel even worse."

Michelle patted his arm. "Why don't we all do it after the game?"

"Aren't we going for pizza?" Jack asked.

"We can do it after that."

Jack groaned. "Do we *all* have to go?"

"Yes, it will be fun," Michelle said.

"Mom, you are the only person who thinks yard work is fun," Jack moaned.

Beth looked through the rearview window and asked, "Can we plant flowers?"

"That's a great idea."

Jack slumped down in the seat. "Some Saturday this is turning out to be."

It was after two before they pulled into Clarence and Edith's driveway. Jeff and Jack had unhooked the mower from the trailer when the elderly couple came around the side of the house.

"What brings you here today?" Clarence pointed to the mower.

"We're your yard crew." Jeff grinned. "Put us to work."

Jeff slipped his arm around Michelle's waist. "I would like for you to meet my wife, Michelle..." He waved Jack and Beth over. "...And our kids."

Edith stepped around her walker and wrapped Michelle in a bear hug. "We have heard so much about you."

Michelle hugged her back. "As I have you."

Clarence came around and embraced her, too.

Michelle squeezed Edith's hand and said, "We have a surprise for you in the truck."

Edith clasped her hands together. "I love surprises."

Beth ran to the back of the vehicle and climbed into the truck bed. "Hey Jack, come help me." She picked up a box filled with petunias of different colors.

Edith grabbed Michelle's arm. "They're for me?"

"Yes." Michelle patted her hand.

Beth handed the first box to Jack and then passed her mother another one filled with impatiens.

"How about we line them up in the driveway, then we can decide where we're going to put them?"

When Beth leaned down for another box, Edith's voice cracked with joy. "There's m-m-more?"

"Yes," Michelle said. "We also have snapdragons, vincas and gaillardias."

Jack started passing them with a second box of petunias, but Edith reached out to stop him. "Put it right here," she said, patting the seat on her walker. She gently touched the flower petals. "I've never seen yellow ones before. Where did you get them?"

"Mom grows them," Beth said proudly.

"You grew all of these?"

"We have a greenhouse," Jack answered matter-of-factly.

Beth handed the last box to her brother and hopped down from the truck.

Jack placed the tray of vincas alongside the other flowers, then wiped his hands on his jeans. "Looks like you're done with me. I'm going to do men's work." With that, he took off running toward his father and Clarence.

"What a charming young man," Edith said.

Beth put her hand over her mouth and giggled.

"So where do you want to plant these?" Michelle asked.

Edith looked around her front lawn. "There was a time this yard was full of flowers."

"Yes, I remember."

"You do?"

"When I was a little girl, we used to drive by here, and I remember thinking it was the most beautiful yard in the world. From spring to the end of fall, your property was alive with color."

Edith held her hands to her chest. "Gardening always brought me such joy."

"I could tell."

"And now I can't get down to do it." Edith chuckled. "Well, I suppose I could get down... I just can't get back up."

Michelle laid a hand on Edith's arm. "We could help you get back up."

Edith clapped her hands in delight. "Would you?" She started walking away. "I have tools in the shed."

Michelle stopped her. "We brought tools." She nodded at her daughter and asked, "Will you get the gloves out of the truck, while I carry the garden tools?"

For a few minutes they watched the guys work. Clarence and Jack were each on a riding mower, while Jeff weed-eated around the porch.

Once he was finished, Michelle said, "Looks like that porch is ready for our magic." She pointed to the flowers. "What would you like to plant there, Edith?"

"The impatiens."

Michelle placed a tray of impatiens on Edith's walker seat before grabbing a rake and her bucket of garden tools. "Time to play in the dirt."

Edith's face lit with joy.

It only took Beth and Michelle a few minutes to rake the beds in front of the porch. When they were finished Michelle turned to Edith. "Ready to get your hands dirty?"

"Oh, yes."

Michelle placed a kneeling pad on the ground and helped Edith get settled. With a trowel in hand, Edith attacked the ground like a child playing in dirt. When Michelle handed her the first flowers to plant, Edith grinned from ear to ear. She patted the soil around them when she was done and leaned back to admire the view. "It is so beautiful." She looked up at Michelle and added, "Thank you. You will never know how much this means to me."

Michelle kneeled down beside the older woman and squeezed her hands. "I think I have an idea." Michelle wiped a tear from Edith's cheek. "I believe we are kindred spirits… the ground calls to us."

"Yes, it does."

Michelle put both hands into the dirt and came up with a handful. She drew it to her face and sniffed. "The smell of earth brightens my day."

"You sniffing dirt again?" Jeff asked, coming up behind her.

She laughed and dropped the handful to the ground.

"I put the thermos of water here on the steps with some paper cups for you ladies." He poured a cup and handed it to Edith. "We're almost done in the front yard, so if you need us, we'll be around back."

As Jeff walked away, Edith said, "That is a mighty fine man you have there."

"He sure is." Michelle watched her husband. Just before he rounded the corner, he turned and winked at her. She blew him a kiss. With a laugh, she focused back on the ground. "This is really good soil."

"It sure is." Edith puffed out her chest. "Back in the day, I used to win first place every year for my garden."

"Every year?" Beth asked.

Edith sat back and laughed. "I'll tell you a little secret. It's horse manure."

Beth dropped her trowel. "Horse poop?" She looked at her hands in disgust.

"Every spring, Clarence would mix it into the dirt, and the flowers loved it."

Michelle laughed at the expression on her daughter's face. "Sweetie, we do the same thing."

"You mean I've been playing in horse poop?"

"What do you think happens to the pile we get from the barn? After a while it turns into dirt, and voila... beautiful flowers."

Beth stared at her gloved hands. "Thank goodness I use gloves." She pointed to Edith and her mother. "But you don't."

The women both dug their hands deep into the dirt and burst out laughing at the look of horror on Beth's face. "You go ahead and use gloves. Us farm girls are happy without."

Together they made quick work of planting the impatiens. When they were finished there, they planted petunias down the sidewalk before putting the other flowers in a bed in the middle of the yard. It was hard but enjoyable work.

When they finished, Edith said, "My yard is beautiful again."

Michelle squeezed her hand. "I promise you we'll keep it looking like this."

Chapter 11

"Mommy," Jack whispered.

Michelle opened her eyes. "What is it?"

He wrapped his arms around her. "It's a good day."

The boy's father rolled over to look at the clock. "Jack, it's four o'clock in the morning. Go back to bed."

Her son kissed Michelle's cheek and squeezed her tighter. "It's a good day."

"Yes, it is. It's the last day of school." Michelle lifted the covers and tucked him in beside her. "And if you don't go back to sleep, you'll miss it."

"No, it's a good day because you aren't going to die."

"What?" Michelle whispered in surprise.

"Today is three months... and you aren't dead."

"That doesn't mean—" Jeff started to say.

Michelle reached out and put a hand on his arm to stop him. "Jack, why do you think that?"

"Because the doctor said three months, but you're still alive, and we pray every day and every night that you won't die. So the doctor was wrong and God was right. You are all better and you're not going to die after all."

"Oh, Jack." Michelle lay her head on his. She didn't have the heart to tell him the truth. She wasn't better. She wasn't worse, but she wasn't better.

"So now we can go on the boys' camping trip."

"Of course you can," Michelle said. "My health doesn't affect that."

"Daddy said we couldn't go because you might die while we're gone."

"What!" Michelle sat straight up. Anger filled her. She glared at her husband. "He said what?"

"Michelle." Jeff touched her shoulder, but she shrugged his hand off.

"Jack, go back to your room. I will come tuck you in, in a few minutes." She waited, then got up and shut their door.

"How dare you say that to him?"

"Michelle"

"You lied to me. You said you couldn't go because you had to finish the Columbia house."

"I do."

"But that isn't the real reason, is it?"

"No."

She paced the floor, trying to rein in her anger. "So all this time you've been focusing on my death, not my living. You really don't believe that God still performs miracles."

He went to her, trying to pull her into his arms. She pulled away.

"Listen to me."

"I thought you had faith." She stormed out of the room. Jeff followed her. He waited while she went into

Jack's room and kissed him goodnight. When she came out, she glared at him, then went downstairs.

He started down the stairs after her.

"Go back to bed, Jeff. I don't want to talk to you right now."

"What about our rule to never go to bed angry?"

At the bottom of the stairs, she spun back toward him. "Angry? I am beyond angry. How dare you put that burden on our son?" She stormed into the kitchen, went straight to the refrigerator and tore the Bible verse off the door. "Do you ever bother to read this?" She waved the paper in his face, reciting it by heart. "*I will not die but live, and will proclaim what the LORD has done.* Did you find this to spread false hope? Because obviously you don't believe it." She ripped it up and flung it in the trash.

"Michelle. Calm down. The doctor said you aren't supposed to get upset." He grasped her around the waist in an attempt to pull her into his arms. She tried to yank away, but he wouldn't let go. "I'm sorry." Jeff kissed the top of her head. "You have to understand. I'm so scared of losing you." He brushed her hair with his fingers. "Yes, I believe in miracles. But we both know God doesn't always answer prayers the way we want Him to."

"Where is your faith?"

"It's there... just not as strong as yours."

She wiped the tears from her face. "The two of you are going."

"How could I live with myself if I went away and you died here all alone?" He choked on a sob. "I couldn't bear it."

"And how do you think I would feel the whole weekend knowing that because of me, you and Jack are missing out on something you both love?" She shook her head. "It's life as usual... until it's not." She looked up at him. "We have to believe." She put her arms around her husband. "God will not allow me to die while you are away. I just know it." They stood there clinging to each other, both silently praying for a miracle.

Michelle pulled away first. "Might as well start the coffee."

Jeff nodded. He squeezed her shoulder. "I love you."

"I love you, too."

Then he turned to leave. "I better get dressed before the kids find me in my underwear."

"Good idea." Michelle sat down at the island and put her head into her hands. She now knew why the doctor had cautioned her about getting upset. Her head was throbbing. She prayed, "Jack is so excited about it being three months. Please, Lord, don't let today be the day. Please don't crush his joy." The teapot whistled and she made herself a cup of tea. She also poured a glass of water and swallowed a pill.

When she heard Jeff coming back downstairs, she fixed his coffee.

He took a sip. "Needed that." Then he kissed her cheek. "You're the best." He nodded toward the French doors. "Looks like another beautiful day. Should we read our Bible outside today?"

"Yes."

They settled side by side on the patio loveseat. Jeff nodded toward the east of the yard. "Look, the sun is starting to peek over the hill."

Michelle softly smiled. "God's promise of another day."

"Thank you, Jesus." Jeff took her hands and held them in his and prayed, "Dear Heavenly Father, I need to ask both You and Michelle for forgiveness." Michelle squeezed his hand. "I do believe in the power of Your healing, just sometimes my worry gets the best of me. Please help me be strong. Give me the faith I need to do as You would have me do. Amen."

Michelle leaned over and kissed him. "I forgive you. Please forgive me for not thinking about how you are feeling. I seem to forget this isn't all about me. That this tumor affects everyone else, too."

Jeff opened the Bible and read aloud. When he finished the chapter, they bowed their heads and prayed for guidance for the day.

Michelle stood up first. "It's the last day of school, so I'm sure the kids will be up before they need to be."

"Jack's little early morning wake-up might keep him sleeping longer."

"You think?" No sooner were the words out of her mouth than Jack and Beth came running down the stairs.

"It's a good day," Jack said jumping around.

"Yes it is," Michelle and Jeff replied at once.

Jack nudged Beth, "You know why it's a good day?"

"Yeah! It's the last day of school."

"No, Mommy's not going to die."

Beth's eyes widened. "Really?" She looked at Michelle with hopeful eyes.

"We need to talk about that," Jeff said.

"But not today." Michelle hugged both of her children to her. "Today is a good day. No one is going to die today. I feel it right here." She pointed to her heart. "God is great. Hallelujah."

The kids danced around the room saying, "Hallelujah."

Michelle finally shooed them out of the room. "Now go get dressed while I make the French toast."

Once he heard their footsteps fading upstairs, Jeff turned to her. "You want Jack to believe you're better?"

"Just until you come back from your camping trip. He won't go if he knows I'm not healed. So for now, let him be happy."

"I still don't—"

"You are going," Michelle said firmly. She patted his hand. "I won't be alone. You know the second you leave, the girls will be taking over this place. We have a fun weekend planned."

"I know, but..."

"There are no buts. God has this."

Jeff took a drink of coffee. He turned to look out the window at a blue jay sitting on a branch singing. A squirrel ran up the tree heading toward the bird feeder. Nature was coming alive this morning, like it did every day. God was in control. "I have something to do in the office. I'll be back in a few," he said, heading down the hall.

Michelle was busy making breakfast when the kids ran back into the kitchen. "How are we going to get to Hoffman's for ice cream if you can't drive us?" Beth asked.

"She can drive now," Jack assured.

"No, Jack, I can't."

"But..."

"Aunt Annette is going to meet us at the office and take us, then we're all going to come back here and go swimming."

Jack and Beth clapped their hands and hopped around.

"One of you go tell your father that breakfast is ready."

Breakfast was anything but quiet. Michelle was grateful when the kids ran to get their shoes. She started to put the milk back in the refrigerator, but stopped short of opening it. There on the door was her Bible verse. She choked up. "You reprinted it?" she asked, looking over her shoulder toward Jeff.

"I do believe in that verse," he said, taking the milk from her and placing it on the counter. He lowered his lips to hers.

"Aww gross, they're kissing," Jack said.

"I hope someday you will love someone so much that you want to be kissing them, too," Jeff said.

"No way."

Jeff laughed. "I will remind you of that someday."

Michelle felt a tug on her heart. Would she see that day? She silently shouted hallelujah. She believed in miracles.

Chapter 12

Michelle pushed Jeff toward the door. "Jack is already in the truck waiting for you."

"I need to say good-bye to Beth," he said looking up the stairs. "Where is she?" No sooner had he asked, than she came flying down. She jumped the last few steps right into Jeff's waiting arms. "I'm going to miss you, buttercup." He gave her a bear hug, before kissing her on the cheek and putting her down. He turned to Michelle and pulled her into his arms. "And you." He lay his forehead against hers. "I don't—"

"Shh." Michelle put her fingers to his lips. "You need to go."

His arms tightened around her.

"Please, I can't breathe." She coughed.

He loosened his grip but didn't let go. Michelle played with the button on his shirt. She startled when Jack honked the horn. "Go, before he drives off without you."

"I really don't want to."

"I know. But you need to." Without a word, he pulled her back into his arms and kissed her as if it were the last time.

"Dad, let's go. The guys are waiting for us," Jack yelled.

Michelle pulled away from the kiss. "You need to go." She took him by the hand and walked out onto the porch with him. "Everything is going to be alright." She pointed to the sky. "God has this." Then she pushed him toward the steps. "Now go have a great time. We'll see you Sunday afternoon.

Jeff walked backwards to the truck, never taking his eyes off his wife. Before getting in, he blew her a kiss and said, "I love you."

"I love you, too." As the boys pulled away from the house, Michelle turned to her daughter and asked, "How about helping me make a surprise for the girls tonight?"

"Cool. What is it?"

"You'll see." She looked at the clock on the microwave. "We need to hurry. I want it in the oven before Grandma gets here." She went to the pantry. Over her shoulder she said, "You get the cherry pie and eggs out of the fridge, please."

Michelle handed Beth a springform pan and coconut spray. "Take this over to the sink and spray the pan, please."

"Why over the sink?"

"We don't want to end up in the hospital because we fell on a slippery floor."

"Nope, we don't." Beth did as she asked, then brought the pan back to the counter. "Now what?"

"We make the cake batter." They measured the ingredients into the stand mixer. When it was ready, Michelle poured just enough to cover the bottom of the pan. She put the bowl down and winked at Beth. "Now for the fun part." She lifted the pie from its tin, and laid it on top of the cake batter.

Beth's mouth flew open. "Mom, what are you doing?"

Michelle laughed. "I told you it was a surprise cake." She handed Beth the bowl of batter. "Now pour the rest into the pan. Make sure the pie is totally covered."

Beth slowly spread the cake batter over the top.

As she lifted it into the oven, Michelle said, "You can't tell anyone what's inside until we cut it."

Beth stared at the oven door. "Oh man, I hope it tastes good."

"It was on *The Kitchen*, so it must be good." Michelle folded up the box and handed it and the aluminum pie plate to Beth. "Run and hide these in the recycling bin. Make sure to cover them up. We don't want anyone guessing our surprise."

Beth hustled into the garage. When she came back she was grinning. "I shoved them all the way to the bottom." They high-fived each other.

Michelle had barely gotten the cake into the oven when her mother arrived. "You started without me?" Kay asked.

"We just wanted to make something extra special for everyone."

"Oh really," Kay said. "What is it?"

Beth started to giggle. "You'll see."

"How are you feeling?"

"Great. No headache today."

Kay hugged her. "If you do get one..."

Michelle kissed her mother's cheek. "I will go lay down." She squeezed her hand and added, "I promise."

"Do you think this might be too much for you?"

"Mom, we do this every year. Why would this be any different?"

"You never had a—"

Michelle rolled her eyes. "This is a fun weekend. There will be no sad thoughts."

Kay nodded. "What time is everyone arriving?"

"Annette and Kimmy will be here around noon. I think they're bringing Colleen with them so Debbie can come right after work. Jeff's mom should be here shortly and Jason's girlfriend, Heidi, is coming around five."

The sound of the front door opening and closing prompted Kay to say, "That must be Gwen."

Beth ran to greet her other grandmother. Michelle took the bags of groceries from Gwen, then gave her mother-in-law a hug.

"How are you feeling?"

She knew folks were concerned, but for once she wished that wasn't the first question everyone asked. "Fine," Michelle replied.

Kay laughed. "That's the first thing I asked, too."

Michelle rolled her eyes. "Maybe I ought to put a sign on the door. *I Am Fine.*"

Beth giggled. "Mom, you are so funny."

Michelle poured Kay and Gwen a cup of coffee, then made cups of tea for her and Beth. Michelle nodded toward the bags Gwen had brought. "Does anything need to be refrigerated?"

"No, it's just the toppings for ice cream sundaes and stuff to make our favorite cookies. The butter needs to be softened anyway." Reaching into one of the bags, she pulled out a pan of homemade cinnamon buns. "And of course our favorite breakfast."

"Yummy." Beth reached for the box. "Can we have one now?"

"Of course," Gwen said.

"Why don't we go out to the patio and eat them?" Michelle suggested.

There was a slight breeze that carried the scent of roses. They sat chatting and laughing. "It is so beautiful out here." Gwen patted Michelle's hand. "I know I say that every time we sit on your patio, but I can't help it. You have done such a great job with the gardens."

"Thank you."

Michelle's cell phone rang. Picking it up she said, "It's Jeff." She rolled her eyes at the phone and answered the call by announcing, "I'm fine."

"I'm just checking."

"You haven't even been gone two hours." It took a few more minutes for her to assure him she was fine. He called again a few hours later.

The day passed by with a lot of laughter. Between swimming and talking, they made cookies, and for dinner, pizza.

They were just cleaning up the dinner dishes, when the phone rang again. "Jeff, stop worrying. Everything is fine," she said. Then she held the phone out. "Everyone, tell him I'm good."

Together the women and girls shouted, "She's fine."

Michelle started to laugh. "I might have a headache from that shouting, but other than that I'm great. Now please go back to your campfire."

She placed the phone on the counter beside her. "Who's ready for dessert?" Michelle asked.

Everyone said at once, "Me."

Michelle took the cover off the cake.

"Yum, that looks good. What kind is it?" Debbie asked.

"Cherry."

"Cherry cake?" Kay questioned. She immediately went to the refrigerator. "Michelle, but where's the cherry pie we bought yesterday?"

Beth started to giggle.

"You sure we bought one?" Michelle said slyly.

"Yes." Her mother continued shifting food around on the shelves. She shut the refrigerator door and started toward the garage. "Did you put it in the extra fridge?"

"No, it's not there either," Michelle said, trying to keep a straight face.

Beth couldn't contain her giggles.

"Beth," Kay said with a huff, "did you eat it?"

"No." The child's face was round and her eyes grew really wide.

"Then what's so funny?"

Michelle put the knife into the cake. She held up the first piece so everyone could see.

"The pie is *in* the cake." Beth hopped up and down with glee.

"What!" Kay looked at the cake. "It better taste good."

"We shall see." Michelle passed out a piece to everyone. She lifted her fork and looked around the island. "Are we ready for this?"

They eyed each other, waiting for someone to be the first brave soul to say yes. Beth dove her fork into the cake, "I am."

"One, two," Michelle counted, and at three they all took a bite at once.

"Wow, this is really good," Kay said. "I forgive you for stealing my pie."

They were barely up on Saturday morning when Jeff called again. Michelle couldn't hide her frustration. "Jeff, please, I'm fine. Stop worrying and go have fun." When he rang an hour later, his mother took the phone from Michelle's hand and walked out to the patio by herself. Whatever she said to him, he didn't call back for the rest of the weekend.

Saturday passed in a blur of laughter. That evening there was a slumber party in the family room. They ordered Chinese food, had popcorn, and watched chick flicks. Sunday morning Michelle rose early and cooked a big breakfast. As they all got ready to leave for church, each one hugged her a little tighter than normal. She knew what they were thinking... that this could very well be the last girls' weekend they would have with her. She noticed more than one of them sniffling.

It was early in the afternoon when Jeff and Jack returned home from their boys' weekend. Michelle and Beth met them at the door.

Jack came running in first. He wrapped his arms around Michelle. "I knew you would be okay."

Jeff followed behind and gave her a bear hug.

"As much as I love your hugs, you two smell really bad," she said laughing.

"Someone needs a shower." Beth waved her hand in front of her nose. "Bad."

"We caught fish this morning for us to have for dinner."

"Greeeaat," Beth said, stretching the word to two syllables. She put her finger in her mouth pretending to gag.

"Why don't we help you unload the truck?" Michelle intervened. "Then you can tell us all about your weekend."

"We had a tent, but me and Daddy slept under the stars. We went fishing and hiking." The words just tumbled out of Jack non-stop.

Beth started talking over top of him, telling Jeff everything the girls had done.

"Sounds like you had a great weekend," Michelle said.

"The best," Jack pronounced.

"Here too."

The girls stored the camping stuff in the garage while Jeff carried the cooler into the kitchen. "I'll deal with putting everything away after I shower."

Michelle patted his arm. "Good idea." She turned to Jack. "You, too… in the shower." As they headed upstairs Michelle called after them, "Are you hungry?"

Jeff laughed. "Always."

While the boys were bathing, Michelle fixed sandwiches and poured everyone a glass of peach tea on the patio. She watched as one by one her family joined her outside.

Jack and Beth were trying to out-talk the other, both spilling over with excitement about their weekends. Her heart swelled with joy. This was what life was all about. Building memories to cherish forever. Jeff walked up behind her, putting his arms around her waist, and kissing her neck.

"It was a great weekend."

"Yes, it was."

He lifted a glass of tea and toasted, "Here's to many more."

Her heart skipped a beat. Would this be the last hurrah? She closed her eyes. She would not allow fear to steal this moment.

She tapped her glass to his. "To many more."

Chapter 13

Michelle was sitting on the bed, buckling the straps of her sandals, when Beth knocked on the door. "Mom?"

"You can come in." Michelle glanced up as her daughter entered the room. "Wow, you look absolutely stunning. I'm glad you decided to wear the blue dress." She motioned for Beth to spin around. "I love the way the skirt flares out and the sun catches the tiny rhinestones like twinkling stars."

Beth grinned. "Thanks, but I can't get the bow right." She pointed behind her. "It looks terrible."

Jeff came out of the bathroom and stopped midstride. "Who is this beautiful angel in front of me?"

Beth giggled. "Oh, Daddy."

Jeff winked at her. "I better not see any boys looking at you."

She rolled her eyes at him. Michelle untied the blue ribbon around Beth's waist and redid it. When she was finished, Jeff spun Beth around. "You will be the prettiest girl to ever sing at church."

Beth giggled.

"We need to get going. We want to get there early enough to get good seats," Michelle said. "It's always crowded on youth Sunday."

Jeff put his arm around Beth's shoulder as they walked toward the stairs. "Are you nervous?"

"A little."

Jack came running out of his room holding up earplugs. "I'm ready."

"That's not funny." Beth stomped her foot.

Jack grabbed his stomach laughing, before tossing the earplugs on the bed. "I'm just kidding."

Just as Michelle predicted, the church was already filling up. Her father Frank waved at them when they entered. "We saved seats for you."

Michelle took the cushioned folding chair beside her mother, then Beth sat next to her, with Jack and Jeff finishing up the row.

"Beth, I do believe that shade of blue brings out the color of your eyes," Kay said.

Frank leaned across his wife to pat Beth on the knee. "I am so glad we finally got a singer in the family." He winked at Jack and added, "I'm tired of us tone-deaf people."

Jack mumbled, "I can sing, too." He crossed his arms, leaning back in his seat and glaring at Beth out of the corner of his eye.

Michelle turned around to say hi to Jennifer Carson. Dr. Carson's wife patted Beth on the shoulder and said, "I understand we are in for a real treat today."

When Beth turned around to see Mrs. Carson, the ribbon on her dress slipped over onto Jack's chair.

A few minutes later the youth group started the service. After the opening prayer, the teen leading the music motioned for the youth choir to come forward. All rose except for Beth.

Jack snickered as his sister struggled to stand, but couldn't. Michelle motioned for her to get up.

"I can't," Beth whispered. "Something's wrong."

Jennifer Carson leaned forward. "Hold on a second, your belt is tied to the chair."

Beth looked horrified, tears welling in her eyes. Jennifer untied the ribbon, freeing Beth.

Jack was having a hard time trying not to laugh.

Jeff squeezed the boy's shoulder, then leaned down and whispered something in his ear.

Jack straightened up. Turning to his sister he whispered, "I'm sorry."

Michelle put her arm around the upset girl and pulled Beth into her side. "Take a deep breath and go join the others." She nudged her daughter forward and watched Beth hurry to join the choir.

Scooting over and leaning down, she whispered into Jack's ear, "That was not funny."

The moment they got in the car to go home, Michelle turned to Jack. "What were you thinking, tying your sister to her chair?"

"It was funny."

"No, it wasn't, Jack." Beth turned her head away from him, not wanting to even look at him. "It was mean."

Jack tried not to snicker. "You should have seen your face when you couldn't stand up."

"I am disappointed in you, Jack. This was your sister's big day and you tried to sabotage it."

Jeff reached across the seat for Michelle's hand. "Don't go getting yourself all upset. You know what the doctor said."

"Too late for that."

Jack crossed his arms, "Any other day you would have thought it was funny."

"This wasn't any other day." Michelle glanced back at Beth. "You did an amazing job singing, sweetheart." She glared at her son. "Your father and I will discuss what we think should be done about your behavior." She leaned her head back against the head rest and closed her eyes.

That evening Michelle's headache returned with a vengeance. She bowed her head and thanked God for the previous weekend free of pain.

By morning it seemed to lighten. She was in the pool with the kids, but Shadow started barking and running back and forth along the edge. Suddenly, the dog dove into the pool and swam directly to Michelle. Gently he put his mouth around her wrist and started to swim toward the ladder.

"Okay boy, I'm getting out." She turned to the kids and said, "We need to climb out for a few minutes."

"But, Mom," Jack whined.

"No buts," she insisted. "I need to go in the house and lay down. I'm going to call Grandma, and when she gets here you can swim some more. But not until then. Is that understood?"

Beth and Jack nodded.

She grabbed her cell phone from the patio table and pressed the speed-dial.

"Mom," she said, looking over her shoulder to make sure the kids were out of the pool and not within hearing distance. Then she hastily stepped into the house, closing the French doors behind her. "I think I'm going to have a seizure, please come over."

"What? Why do you think that?"

"Shadow lets me know." She tried to explain her suspicions about the dog's uncanny ability, but her words started to slur. Michelle stumbled to the guest room with Shadow attentively by her side.

"I'll be right there," Kay said and hung up.

Less than three minutes later, the front door opened and Aunt Debbie raced into the house yelling, "Michelle."

"She's laying down in the guest room," Beth said. "What are you doing here?"

"Your grandma called me," she said, hurrying down the hall. She opened the door to the guest room. "Get off the bed," she yelled at Shadow and motioned for the dog to get down. He didn't even look at her.

Debbie started toward the bed to push him off before realizing Michelle's whole body was jerking. She stopped mid-step and a loud ear-piercing sound came from within her.

Jack dashed up behind Beth to the bedroom, but both stopped short at the doorway.

Debbie collapsed to the floor, sobs racking her body. Her voice broke as she motioned for the children to leave the room. Between hysterics she managed to say, "This is it, she's d-d-dying."

Beth rushed past her aunt toward the bed.

"No, get back," Debbie said.

Beth ignored her. "She's just having a seizure. I need to help her."

As she neared the bed, Shadow jumped down. Beth removed the pillow, tossed it on the floor, then knelt on the mattress and rolled her mother onto her side. She remained on the bed, making sure her mother couldn't roll off.

Her aunt's sobbing was getting on her nerves. She wanted to shout at her to get a grip, but knew her mother wouldn't be happy with her if she did. She glanced over her shoulder at Jack who stood speechless at the door. Her brother's eyes were round with fear.

Debbie somehow managed to pulled herself up from the floor. "I need to call 911," she said, fumbling with a cell phone.

"No, you don't. Look, she isn't shaking anymore." Beth calmly rolled her mother onto her back again, then covered her up. "She just needs to sleep it off."

A gasp at the door had every head turn. Jack hurled himself into his grandmother arms. "She's dying," he sobbed.

Kay held him tight. Beth pushed hair from her mother's face, then looked up at her grandmother. That's when her own tears started. "Mommy had a seizure."

Kay moved toward the bed, bringing Jack with her. She patted Shadow's head. "Good boy." Then she brushed Michelle's forehead.

Beth looked at the door where her aunt was still in a frenzy. "Mom really just needs quiet." Next she looked from her brother up to her grandmother. "And I think he really needs you."

"Yes, I think you are right." Kay kissed the top of Beth's head. "What about you?"

In a small voice, Beth said, "I'm okay." She sat down on the chair beside the bed. "I'm going to stay here until she wakes up."

Kay nodded then knelt down in front of Jack. "Your Mom is going to be okay now," she whispered. He grabbed hold of her as if afraid to let go.

She guided both Debbie and Jack into the family room and pulled Jack onto her lap. He buried his face into her shoulder. "Oh sweetie, I know how scared you must have been seeing your mom having a seizure, but she's alright now."

His whole body went rigid. "No, she isn't. She's going to die and it's all my fault." He jumped up and ran from the living room then flew up the stairs to his bedroom.

Kay hurried after him.

"Unfortunately, he's right," Debbie said, wiping her face with her sleeve. "She's dying."

Kay stopped midstride, turned, and glared at Debbie. "What do you think Michelle would say if she heard you say that?"

Debbie hung her head.

"I need to go talk to Jack. Thank you for coming so quickly."

"Of course." Debbie followed Kay to the hallway then said, "I need to get back to work."

Beth was relieved when she heard Aunt Debbie open the front door and leave. Her grandmother's footsteps went softly up the stairs. Beth continued to sit in the chair beside her mother's bed, singing softly.

A movement from the side caused Beth to glance up. Her father was standing in the doorway. Relief flooded through her as she ran to him. He pulled her into his arms. "Oh Daddy, I was so scared."

"I know, baby." He went to the bed and brushed Michelle's hair from her face. "Where's your grandmother?"

"I'm here," Kay called.

Jeff looked up as she entered the room behind them. "What happened?"

"We should go into the kitchen and give Michelle some quiet," Kay said.

At the door, they all gave a glance toward the bed, where Beth had tucked the pillow back under her mother's head. Michelle's face was almost as white as the pillow case. They lingered a moment more, each holding on to hope.

Once they were settled around the kitchen table Jeff asked again, "What happened?"

Beth told them about being in the pool and how Shadow practically dragged Michelle out. Kay added that Michelle called her to tell her what was going on.

"When I asked why she thought she was going to have a seizure, she said Shadow told her."

"Shadow?" Jeff asked, one eyebrow arched.

"That's what she said, then her speech started to slur. Since I was further away, I thought it was best to get Debbie here." Kay frowned. "I know she's your brother's wife, but never in all my life have I wanted to punch someone."

Jeff looked shocked. "Why?"

"When I came in, she was standing in the doorway screaming, 'Michelle is dying,' at the top of her lungs." The older woman squeezed Beth's hand. "You ought to be so proud of your daughter. She's the one who took care of Michelle."

Jeff reached across the table for his daughter's hand. "You did?"

Beth nodded.

"But how did you know what to do?"

Beth pointed to her tablet sitting on the bookshelf in the family room. "I googled *seizures*."

"How did you have time?"

"Not today, Daddy. I did it when Mom was in the hospital, just in case I ever needed to know what to do."

Jeff looked at Kay. "Did you think to do that?" Michelle's mother shook her head. "Neither did I. Beth, you are so smart." He pulled her into a bear hug.

"Mom, what are you doing here?"

They turned in surprise at Michelle's voice.

Walking into the kitchen, Michelle glanced at the clock. "Jeff, why are you home so early?"

Jeff rushed to her. "You feeling okay?"

"Yes, just a little tired." She looked at them ogling her like a side-show freak. "What's going on? Why was I sleeping in the guest room?"

"You had another seizure," Jeff said.

Michelle sank down into a chair at the table. "I did?"

Beth jumped up and put her arms around her mother. "I was so scared."

"I'm so sorry you had to see that, baby." Michelle looked around. "Where's Jack?"

"Sleeping," Kay said. "The umm... stress wore him out."

Michelle rubbed Beth's back. "I'm so sorry."

"It's not your fault." Kay patted her hand. "I am so proud of Beth. She took care of you the whole time."

"You did?" Michelle hugged her little girl tight.

"Mommy." Jack choked on a sob, as he came running into the room. "You're not d-d-dead." Tears streamed down his face. Michelle rose and went to him, pulling him into her arms.

"No, baby, I'm not dead." Her tears mingled with his. "I just had a seizure."

"But..." he looked into her eyes, "...Aunt Debbie said you were dying."

Michelle looked at Kay. Kay did nothing but shake her head. "I promise you I will never call that woman again."

Michelle sat back at the table, pulling Jack down on her lap. Shadow followed them, lying down beside Michelle's chair.

She reached down and petted the dog.

"What did you mean," Kay asked, "when you said Shadow told you that you were going to have a seizure?"

"When did I say that?"

"Don't you remember calling me?"

"No." Michelle shook her head. "The last thing I remember was fixing lunch."

"About Shadow..." Jeff said.

"I can't be sure, but I think the dog knows when I'm going to have a seizure. He starts to hover, and won't let me near anything that could hurt me, like the stove, the stairs." She looked down and realized she was in her bathing suit. "And I'm guessing the pool."

"How many times has this happened?" Jeff stared at her.

"A few."

"How many times is a few?"

"I don't know... maybe four."

Kay gasped. Jeff leaned across the table, looking her right in the eyes. "You mean to say you have had four other seizures and didn't feel the need to tell me?"

"What was I supposed to say... I think I might have had a seizure today?"

Jeff pushed back his chair, almost knocking it over when he stood up. "Yes."

"I didn't want you to worry."

"Really, Michelle. What kind of lame excuse is that?" He stormed out of the house.

"You should have told him," Kay advised.

"I–"

"No, you should have told him."

Michelle nodded. She lifted Jack from her lap and kissed the top of his head. "I need to go talk to Daddy."

She stood too quickly and her legs almost gave out. She was tired and just wanted to go back to bed, but the need to talk to her husband was stronger. She put on a brave face and stepped out on the patio to face the music. He wasn't there. She looked toward the barn and followed the path. She found him brushing one of the horses. She walked up behind him and placed her hand over his. "I'm sorry. I should have told you."

"Yes, you should have." He pulled her to him. "We're supposed to be in this together. No secrets."

"I know. I just didn't want you to worry."

"Michelle, you can't keep me from worrying about you." He kissed her forehead. "I worry every second of every day. Each time the phone rings, I worry... is this the call?" He held her face between his hands. "How can I help you if I don't know what's going on?"

"To be honest, I didn't know for sure."

"How can you not know?"

"If Beth hadn't told me I had a seizure today, I wouldn't have known. I woke up tired and disoriented, with no memory of anything that happened the hours before. I just sort of assumed that's what happens."

"Promise me, no more secrets."

"I promise."

Chapter 14

Sunday morning, Michelle looked up from setting the table as Beth padded into the kitchen, still in her pajamas. Jeff was cooking his mystery breakfast.

"Jack won't get up. He said he isn't going to church today."

"Of course he's going to church," Michelle scoffed.

"He said God isn't real and you can't make him go."

Michelle's eyes flashed to her husband.

"I'll go talk to him," Jeff said, putting the spatula down.

"You need to finish cooking." Michelle handed the napkins to Beth and directed, "You finish setting the table and I'll go talk to him."

When she entered her son's room, Jack pulled the covers over his head. His muffled voice sounded like he was murmuring into his pillow. "I'm not going. And you can't make me."

"No, I won't make you go." She sat on the edge of the bed. "We go to church because we look forward to rejoicing with God every week, not because we're forced to go." Pulling the covers from his face, she added, "But I need to know why you don't want to go, when you love it so much."

"Because God isn't real."

"Oh no, Jack, that isn't true."

"Then he's a liar."

"You know that isn't true either."

"It is." Jack sat up in bed, hugging his knees to his chest.

"Why do you think that?"

"The Bible says 'ask and ye shall receive'. And I keep asking for God to take that tumor out of your brain, but He doesn't."

"You know He doesn't answer all prayers the way we want Him to."

"Then He lies."

"No, Jack. He doesn't."

Jack reached over to his nightstand and picked up a card with a mustard seed on it. "It says right here, if you have as much faith as a grain of mustard, then you can tell the mountain to move... and it will. Well, I have that much faith, but you're still dying."

Michelle wrapped her arms around him and hugged her son tight. "I know it seems like He isn't listening, but He is. The doctor said it seemed that I wouldn't be here more than three months, yet it's been almost four. Don't you think that's an answer to our prayers?"

Jack pushed away from her. "You had a seizure because God's mad at me."

"Whaaaat!"

"I tied Beth to the chair and now God's mad at me and isn't going to answer our prayers because of me." Jack pulled the covers back over his head.

Michelle tried to pull them down, but his grip was too tight. She got up and walked around to the other side of the bed, then crawled in under the covers.

He stared wide eyed at her. She wiped the tears from his face with her fingers. "Jack, God is not mad at you."

"I was bad."

"Bad isn't the right word. Mischievous, yes." Michelle squeezed Jack's hand. "Do you think God is mad at Granddad?"

"No." Jack gave his mother a puzzled look.

"Why not? Granddad does crazy things all the time." Michelle thought for a moment then grinned. "How about Grandpa telling you to pull his finger in church? If anything would make God mad, it was that."

Jack wiped his nose with his sleeve. "Yeah."

"Don't you think God has a sense of humor?"

"I never thought about it."

"Well, He must because he made Granddad, didn't He."

Jack's mouth fell open. "I'm telling him you said that."

"I'm sure God reacted the same way your dad and granddad did when Beth couldn't get up out of her chair. He probably tried to hide his amusement behind a stern face." It was becoming uncomfortable so she pulled the covers down, uncovering their faces. Taking a deep breath she said, "Now, isn't this better?"

He lowered his head. "I don't want you to die."

She wiped a tear from her son's cheek. "Everyone dies, and whether I die today or fifty years from now, it's still going to devastate you. When that day comes, I want you to remember always how much I love you. And I need you to know that God is still God, no matter what happens in life that we don't like."

"Well, He might not be mad at me, but I'm mad at Him."

"It's okay to be mad at God for a little bit. He still loves you."

Jack toyed with his comforter. Not looking at her, he asked, "How do you know?"

"Remember last week when you were mad at me because I wouldn't drive you to Shawn's house to play?"

Jack hid his face between his knees.

"You were mad at me, but I wasn't mad at you. I still loved you with all my heart. Just like God does." She rubbed his hair. "He knows sometimes things are just too much for us, and we need to scream at Him. He just patiently waits for us to come back to Him."

"I don't want to be mad at God."

"I know."

"But why doesn't He heal you? He could if He wanted, but He doesn't."

"We don't know that he won't heal me. Until I take my last breath, there's still hope."

"It's not fair."

"Life is not always fair." Michelle started to get up from the bed.

Jack held onto her arm. "I don't want you to die."

She held him tight as he sobbed.

"I don't want you to give up hoping for a miracle, but I also need you to remember that sometimes God doesn't answer our prayers the way we want. That doesn't mean He doesn't love us. Bad things do not come from God."

"But He could fix it."

"And that's why we keep praying."

Jack looked up at his mother. "I'm scared."

Michelle nodded. Before glancing out the window she said, "I'm scared, too."

"You are?"

"Yes, not of dying, because I know I will be with Jesus. I'm scared of what my dying will do to you and Beth and Daddy. It hurts me to know I am going to cause you so much pain." She wiped the tears from her son's face. "Being scared and mad is what happens when we focus on the tumor. And that's why I try my best to only concentrate on this moment that God has given us. Every moment of every day is a gift and I want to savor each second. I don't want to stress about what's going to happen. There will be time for that when it happens. But right now, while things are good, that's what I want to think about." She kissed the top of his head. "Every morning when I open my eyes, I say hallelujah, and anytime throughout the day I find my mind wandering into tumorville..." She smiled when Jack gave her a funny look, then added, "...That's what I call the tumor and all the bad feelings that come with it."

Jack giggled. "Mommy, sometimes you are so silly."

Michelle tickled him. "Yes, I am. So when tumorville decides to entice me to visit, I just say hallelujah."

"I tried that," Jack said. "It didn't work."

"You know why I picked hallelujah to say?"

"No."

"It means 'praise the Lord'. And when you say it, you feel it in your heart."

"I don't."

Michelle stood up, pulling Jack from the bed. "Then let me show you how to say it when things are really, really scary." She took a big breath and said, "Hallelujah." She looked at Jack. "You say it with me."

He begrudgingly mumbled, "Hallelujah."

"Well, no wonder it doesn't work. You have to say it like you mean it." She spun around with her hands in the air. "Hallelujah!"

She grabbed Jack's hands and started to twirl him around with her, saying, "Hallelujah," with joy.

He began to laugh. "It does work."

She knelt down in front of him. "When I say hallelujah, in my mind, I'm spinning around with my hands in the air, praising God for all He's done for me. And it makes my heart sing. When my heart is full of God's love, how can I be sad?"

Jack played with a lock of his mother's hair. "I'm sorry I was mad at God."

"Let's pray and tell God that." They knelt beside the bed and Jack prayed, "Dear Heavenly Father, I'm sorry I was mad at you and called you a liar. I know that isn't true. I was just so scared. I don't want my mom to die. Please heal her tumor."

Michelle added, "Please give us the strength to deal with whatever lays ahead. Thy will be done. Amen." Michelle hugged Jack. "You ready to go eat Daddy's mystery breakfast?"

Jack made a face. "It isn't Brussel sprouts pancakes again, is it?"

Michelle laughed. "No. I learned my lesson. There will never again be leftover Brussel sprouts in the fridge on Sunday morning."

"Thank goodness." They both laughed.

Jack raced down the stairs and into the kitchen. "What's the mystery today?"

"Pretty boring, just scrambled eggs with leftover veggies and lunch meat." Jeff winked at Michelle. "I think someone cleaned out the fridge yesterday."

"I promise I did not."

"*Hmph.*" He dipped out the eggs onto their plates. "It was slim pickings in there."

The kids forked through the eggs, trying to see what he had put in them. They named the ingredients as they found them. "Eggs, onions, broccoli."

Then Beth pulled out something green. "What's this stuff?"

"Lettuce," Jeff said happily.

Michelle chuckled. "Lettuce, really?" She shook her head. "Is nothing safe from you?"

"Nope. You know the deal. Mystery breakfast is made with whatever I find." He grinned. "There is also bacon and tomato. So it's a BLT with a twist."

They all laughed. The kids cautiously took their first bite. "Umm... it's pretty good," Jack said.

"You act surprised."

"They still haven't gotten over the Brussel sprout pancakes."

He grinned. "They weren't awful, just weird."

"They were weird, alright," Jack said between bites.

Halfway through breakfast, Michelle put down her fork. "We aren't going to church today."

"What!" the others said at once.

"Why not?" Jeff asked.

"Oh, don't worry. We won't be leaving God out of this day. We'll just worship him in a different way."

"How?" Jeff asked.

"I would like for us to go to Luray Caverns and see firsthand how God works beneath the surface." She looked around the table. "I think it will help us all, not only to feel, but to see the wonders of God's creation."

"But what about church?" Beth glared at her brother.

"It will be just like when we're on vacation and have our own special service."

"Are we going on vacation this year?" Jack asked.

"No," Jeff said at the same time Michelle said, "Yes."

Michelle looked at her husband. "Yes, we are."

Her husband shook his head adamantly.

"We'll talk about that later. For now, I feel in my heart that God wants us to go on this little trip today."

"Then that's what we'll do."

"We'll take a picnic lunch and eat up on Skyline Drive." Michelle's smile lit up the whole room. "It will be a glorious day." She got up from the table and said, "After you put your dishes in the sink, Jack, go get the cooler from the garage, and Beth, you can get the picnic basket."

"What are we going to eat? Daddy used all the leftovers," Jack said.

"Not *all.*" Michelle winked. She opened the refrigerator and shifted the milk and juice bottles to get to a container of potato salad. "We can stop at Royal Farms and get some chicken. Jeff, can you get the large thermos? It's on the top shelf right inside the garage."

She quickly packed the picnic basket with paper plates, cups, plastic ware, and snacks. She put the potato salad in the cooler along with bottled water. "We'll get ice when we stop for the chicken." She filled the thermos with strawberry lemonade and loaded the dishwasher before heading upstairs to get ready.

Alone in their room Jeff asked, "Is this a good idea?"

"Why wouldn't it be?"

"We umm... we can't take Shadow with us. He isn't allowed in the cavern. What if you have a seizure?"

Michelle finished pulling on her shorts before answering him. "And what if I have a seizure at church? Or at the grocery store, or any number of places we can't take the dog?" She put her hands on her hips. "Are we supposed to stop living, just in case?" She walked over to him and put one hand on his arm. "I know you're worried, but we can't live our whole life in fear."

Jeff wrapped his arms around her, holding her tight. "I know, it's just—"

She placed a finger to his lips. "We live each moment and trust God to see us through."

He lowered his lips to hers. "I love you."

"I love you, too." She gave him one last kiss, then pulled away. "Now let's go see what message God has for us today."

The drive to Luray Caverns was long, but the kids didn't seem to mind. They were on an adventure. They laughed and sang songs.

When they pulled into the parking lot, Jack said, "It just looks like a store."

"That's what's so wonderful about this place. On the surface it looks ordinary, but once we start down under the earth, you'll see firsthand the handiwork of God. I believe that's what God wants to show us today... that even though things may not be the way we hope and we can't see any changes, that doesn't mean He isn't working on our miracle."

No sooner had Jeff parked than Jack started to jump out.

"Grab your sweater! It will be cool underground," Michelle called after him.

Beth's and Jack's eyes grew wide with awe as they descended into the cavern to Dream Lake, where the water mirrored the ceiling.

"Wow, that's so cool," Jack marveled. "It looks like the ceiling is touching the water."

They walked slowly, admiring the rock formations. At the stalactite pipe organ, they stood with the rest of the tour group and listened to the music being played off the rocks.

Jeff reached into his pocket and handed them each a coin. He tossed his into the wishing well and soon the others followed suit. Michelle sensed that each of them was making the same wish—that the tumor would disappear forever.

Jack loved the giant cave and Pluto's ghost.

Beth was excited to see Titania's Veil was the prettiest formation. "It looks just like layers of icicles trying to make a beautiful veil for its bride... the mountain."

Jack slapped his leg. "That's the most ridiculous thing I ever heard."

"Well, that's what it looks like to me." She flipped her hair and walked away from him.

Jack put his hand in his mother's as they continued their journey underground. "This place is really cool, isn't it?"

Michelle looked around her. "It is truly amazing."

They laughed at stones that looked just like fried eggs.

When they came out of the cavern, they were all smiling.

"That was great," Jack said. "Can we go again?"

"No," Jeff answered. "We're going up to Skyline Drive to eat lunch."

"Why don't we just stay here and eat?" Michelle offered, nodding toward some trees. "We could put the blanket down there and eat now. I'm sure everyone is starving."

Jack rubbed his stomach. "I am."

"Me too," said Beth.

"Me three," added Jeff.

As they ate Michelle mused, "It's really hard to imagine we were deep under this very ground. Isn't it amazing how God took the time to make all that beauty when most people won't even see it? If He cares enough to do that with rock, what do you think He's doing in our lives?" She stared up at the clouds. "I'm going to put this in my blessing book." She thought for a minute. "I wonder what color tulip would best represent this day?"

"I think a frilly one," Beth said. "I'm going to plant one, too."

Jeff and Jack both added, "Me too."

"But mine isn't going to be a silly frilly one," Jack said. "Mine's going to be strong."

"Tulips aren't strong," Beth pointed out.

"If they aren't strong, then how do they push up through the ground?" Jack jumped up. "When are we going to go up the mountains?"

Michelle laughed at how fast her son's thoughts could change. "Help clean this stuff up and we'll go now."

Chapter 15

The summer flew by. Life was almost normal. Michelle worked from home as she did every summer. When she had to meet with a client, her mother watched the kids. When Shadow started to hover, Beth had Michelle go lay down in the guest room. When the seizure hit, Beth took care of her. Jack would sit outside the room praying. For two weeks, the whole family took an RV up the east coast to Maine to see the whales, then to Niagara Falls.

Before they knew it, it was September and the start of another school year. When Michelle woke Beth up, her daughter said, "I can't go to school."

Michelle touched Beth's head. "You don't feel warm."

"I'm not sick."

"Then why can't you go to school?"

"Who is going to take care of you when you have a seizure?"

Michelle pulled Beth into her arms. "Oh baby, don't you worry about that. I have Shadow to warn me."

"But..."

"No buts. It's my job to worry about you, not your job to worry about me. If Shadow starts to hover, I promise I will call Grandma right away." Michelle walked over to the closet. "And if you stay home, who will see your beautiful new outfit?"

She laid the black leggings and light pink tunic top with bell sleeves on the bed and smiled.

"This blouse makes me think of Juliet." She ran her fingers though Beth's long blonde hair. "Only you better not fall in love with some boy now that you're in fourth grade."

Beth put her hands over her mouth trying not to giggle. "Oh, Mom."

"My baby is growing up. It seems like yesterday you were just starting school." Michelle gave Beth a lingering hug before quickly leaving the room.

In the hall, she leaned against the wall with a hand clenched to her chest. She fought back the tears wondering if this would be the last first day of school she would share with them. After a deep breath and a silently whispered, "Hallelujah, the Lord is my strength," she could hear movement in Jack's room.

She knocked before opening the door. Jack was slipping on his shoes. "I'm already awake."

"I see that."

"First day of school is always the best."

"Why's that?"

"I get to see my friends I haven't seen all summer."

Michelle nodded. "I made French toast."

Jack rubbed his stomach. "Yummy."

He dashed past her and ran down the stairs, jumping the last three steps.

"Jaaaaaaack!"

He looked sheepishly over his shoulder at her and grinned before hurrying into the kitchen. "Morning, Dad." Jack took a seat at the table, reaching for his glass of milk.

Jeff put down the paper and ruffled Jack's hair. "Morning, sport."

"How did the Orioles do last night?" They talked about their favorite players until Beth and Michelle joined them.

Michelle took the French toast from the oven and put it on the table. Jack reached for the first piece.

Jeff stopped him. "Prayer first, then food."

Jack dropped back into his seat. "Can I say it?"

Jeff nodded.

They bowed their heads. "Dear Heavenly Father, thank you for this day. Thank you for the food we are about to eat. Please keep us safe as we go to school and work. And please take extra care of Mommy today, since we won't be here to help if she needs us. Amen."

Michelle kept her eyes closed an extra few seconds. She felt Jeff's hand on her arm and looked up, trying to keep the tears from falling. With a smile on her face she said, "That was very nice of you, Jack. But you do know I won't be alone, right? Nicole and Shadow will be with me."

"And God," Jack mumbled through a mouthful of food.

"Yes, and God."

They waited in the truck at the end of the driveway for the bus. Jack was the first to see it coming. He leaned over the seat and gave his dad a quick hug before clinging an extra minute to Michelle.

"Have a great day at school." She kissed his cheek.

He jumped out of the truck happily. "Don't work too hard," he said.

Beth wrapped her arms around her mom's neck and laid her head on Michelle's shoulder. "Can't I stay home with you?"

"No."

"You could homeschool me this year."

Michelle got out of the truck and pulled Beth into her arms. "Sweetie, I will be okay." The bus came to a stop and she kissed the top of her daughter's head. "Now go and have a great day. Look... Amanda's waving at you." She wiped the tears from Beth's eyes. "No more worrying. God is in control." Then she gave her daughter a gentle shove. "Go have an awesome day."

She watched the bus pull away with tears streaming down her own cheeks. She hadn't even heard Jeff get out of the truck, but there he was pulling her into his arms. "Is this the last first day of school I'll share with them? Is everything we do the last thing?" Her heart broke with grief for all the first days she would be missing.

Jeff held her tight, rubbing her hair. There was nothing he could say. He had no answer. All he could do was pray for a miracle.

When her tears subsided, he helped her back into the truck. Instead of pulling out of the driveway and into their shop's parking lot, he spun the vehicle around and went home.

"We aren't going to work?" she asked.

"I think we need some time with God first."

He pulled the truck to the side of the house. She climbed out and started toward the door until Jeff took her by the hand.

"We're not going inside. We are going for a quiet walk and let's see how God talks to us."

Hand in hand, they wandered past the pasture. For a few minutes, they watched as the horses frolicked in the fields with their manes blowing in the slight breeze. They whinnied in delight when they saw Jeff and Michelle.

As the couple headed toward the woods, a bunny hopped out of sight. A cardinal and a blue jay flew from tree to tree as if playing tag. The sun peeped through the leaves of the tall oaks, giving them tiny rays of light to guide their way. They sat down on a log and listened to the sound of God's creation.

Michelle kissed Jeff's cheek. "Thank you. I needed this."

He hugged her and said, "Me too." Then they kissed. "We can't ever stop believing in miracles."

She nodded. "I know. And I truly believe that God is working a miracle in me. After all... it's been six months and I'm still fighting. It's just that some days the sadness is the hardest fight."

"And that is why God gave us to each other. So we could fight the darkness together."

The rest of the day sped by. Before Michelle knew it, the kids were bursting through the door of her office at work, each talking over the other and trying to tell about their day. Shadow bounced between the two of them.

Michelle finally raised her hands. "One at a time." She grabbed her purse and nodded to Nicole. "We're going to walk home."

"I can drive you."

Michelle only chuckled. "I think the walk will do them good."

The mile-long driveway didn't seem so long today. The kids excitedly told her about their days. Halfway home, Jack and Shadow took off running. Michelle and Beth continued walking hand in hand. "I'm glad you had such a good day."

"Did you have a good day, too, Mommy?"

"Why, yes I did. I got a lot of work done today."

Beth looked up at her hesitantly. "Any…"

"No." She pointed at Shadow. "He didn't hover at all today." She chuckled. "But Aunt Debbie did. You know it's the first full day back at work, and Nicole and I had to sneak out the back door to go check out one of the jobs."

Beth rolled her eyes. "I bet she wasn't happy when she saw you were gone."

"No, I guess not."

Beth started to run toward Jack, but stopped short. She bent down and picked up a red leaf. "Hey, Jack," she called. "Look what I found… the first color of fall."

Jack and Shadow ran back to them. "Wow, where did that come from?"

They all looked up into the trees. There were no other changing leaves.

Beth hugged it to her. "It's a gift from God. Right, Mom?"

"Yes." The three of them raised their arms to the sky and shouted, "Hallelujah!"

Shadow leaped and barked.

"Even Shadow is praising God," Jack said.

Michelle patted Shadow's head. "He is truly an amazing dog."

By mid-September, it was time to order the tulip bulbs for the fall planting. They each brought their blessing books to the table and picked a catalog to select the tulips they wanted to represent their blessings, each saying what the special moment had been and which type of tulip they wanted.

Beth remained silent.

"Beth, what tulips are you picking?"

She hung her head.

Michelle reached for the child's book, turning it so she could read the entries. "Beth, why did you stop writing down your blessings after March?"

"Because of your tumor."

Michelle turned her own blessing book around so Beth could read it. She pointed to the line where she had written, "Thank you for the tumor."

Beth gasped. "Why would you thank God for your tumor?" She jumped up and smacked her palms on the table. "Do you want to die?"

Michelle stood and reached for her daughter. "No, I don't want to die."

"Then why would you write that?"

"Because of the tumor, now I face each and every day as a gift. I treasure every moment God has given me with all of you. I have grown closer to God. I appreciate the little things that before I took for granted. I wake up each morning saying hallelujah and meaning it. I go to bed each night saying the same thing. So yes, I count the tumor as a blessing. Not because I want to die, or because I like the headaches or the seizures... but because I know that God is granting me a miracle every day I'm still alive. So I'm planting a bunch of wild blue heart tulips for those blessings."

"I didn't put the tumor down as a blessing, but I have put down 365 red tulips... one for each day we have you from the time we first found out about the tumor," Jeff said.

"It hasn't been a year yet," Michelle corrected.

"It will be."

Michelle laughed. "You can't plant ahead. The blessing year goes from October first to September thirtieth. Since we didn't know about the tumor until the end of March, you can't plant that many tulips."

"Yes, I can."

"You can only count the days from March twenty-seventh until October first." She shook her head. "Any days after October have to go on next year's list."

Jeff rolled his eyes and stuck his tongue out at her. "You and your rules."

She laughed again. "Now, Beth, I'm sure you can think of some blessings that happened after March, can't you?"

Beth shrugged and sat back down.

"What about this one of mine? 'Beth knew what to do when I have a seizure.' You could thank God for giving you the insight to google what to do."

Jeff said, "That was a blessing," and Jack nodded his agreement.

Beth grinned and wrote it down. "I think I will plant the Lilac Wonder for that, since I was wondering what a seizure was." She pointed to a picture in the catalog of a purple tulip with a bright yellow center.

"That is beautiful," Michelle said.

"I'm planting the Orange Emperor for the Orioles."

Beth rolled her eyes at her brother. "You plant that every year."

"Cause I love them."

"You can't love them. You don't even know them."

"Yes, I do." Jack looked at his Dad. "Can't I love them?"

"You most certainly can. I love them, too."

"*Hmph.*"

Michelle said, "I'm planting Angel tulips for Shadow." They all agreed they each needed to plant some for him.

Making their way around and around the table, they shared their blessings and named the tulip they were planting for it.

Shadow got up and walked to the door. Jack started to jump up. Michelle put her hand out and said, "I'll let him out." She patted the dog on the head as he went out the open door.

She stood for a moment, watching him run up the path. She gazed at the heart in the center of the hill. How many tulips would be needed to fill it, and this entire bank?

She leaned against the door frame. They had started this tradition ten years ago and they weren't even halfway to filling it. She quickly wiped a tear from her eye. How much time did she have left? Would she even see the spring?

Shadow came bounding back toward her. He jumped up and licked her face.

Michelle gently pushed him down. "Boy, what did you do that for?" She wiped the slobber off her face. She turned to look at her family, happily counting their blessings, and her heart filled with joy. This is what life was all about, treasured memories. She went back to the table wondering what blessing tomorrow would bring.

Chapter 16

The bulbs arrived and it was time to plant. Every evening after dinner, they quickly went to work putting them in the ground. Michelle plastered a smile on her face as she dug her first hole.

Jeff knelt down beside her and nudged her shoulder with his. "What's wrong?"

"Nothing."

He raised an eyebrow, sensing what she was thinking. She lowered her head and twisted her tool into the ground. Jeff put a finger under her chin and raised her head to look directly into her eyes. "Talk to me."

She wiped a tear from her cheek, leaving a smudge of dirt in its place. "I can't keep from thinking that this very well could be the last time I plant tulips." She waved her hand from one side of the bank to the other. "I don't think I will live to see this whole hill come alive with love."

"Of course you will." He looked over at the kids busy planting their bulbs. "With four of us planting our blessings every year, it will take no time to fill this bank."

She shook her head. "You know this could be the last—"

"We don't think like that."

"But—"

"No buts. We believe in miracles. And this time next year, you will be out here side by side with me."

"I want to believe that," she bit her lower lip, "but we don't know when God will decide the miracle of my life will end."

"No, we don't. Just like we don't know when any of our lives will end. It's a day by day gift." He took her hand in his. "We believe in miracles. Hallelujah."

"Hallelujah," she repeated and smiled timidly. "This time next year we'll be planting the rest of your red tulips."

He leaned over and kissed her. "Speaking of red tulips, I better get busy planting these." He pointed to the large pile of bulbs inside the heart.

She shook her head. "That looks like an awful lot of tulips there."

"I played by the rules... there are only 190 ... one for each day within your guidelines."

"You actually counted the days?"

"I know you and your rules." He squeezed her hand. "So yes, I counted them."

She glanced at the pile and said, "Glad that's your pile and not mine."

He winked. "One for every day God has heard our prayers." He put a hand over his heart. "I feel right here that He will continue to answer them." He leaned over, kissing her softly before standing up and moving to his mound. As he planted the first, his heart clenched with fear. Just how many red bulbs would he get to plant next year? Yes, God had granted them six months with minimum change in their life. But he sensed that was about to change.

Jeff glanced over at his wife and noticed how her hand shook ever so slightly. He had also noticed the bruises on her legs and arms from when she bumped into things. No, she hadn't said anything, but he had noticed the changes in her.

And they were not good.

Jeff wanted to believe God would heal his wife, but he had to face reality—He might not. If this was their last year together, Jeff was going to make sure her dream came true. Come spring, this hill would be covered with tulips.

Jeff wiped a tear from his face and carefully placed another bulb in the ground. He glanced over at Michelle happily digging in the dirt. He watched her for a few minutes.

"Hey, those bulbs aren't going to plant themselves," she said when she caught him staring at her.

He grinned. "No, they won't." He lowered his head and got back to planting. He smiled to himself. Little did she know of the surprise he had hidden in the barn.

He looked up at the sky. *Please God, don't take her from us.* His heart believed she would be healed, but his brain was telling him otherwise. He planted another bulb. *Like Michelle is so fond of saying, until she takes her last breath, there is still time for a miracle. We really need that miracle.* With a heavy heart, he continued to plant.

They worked for about an hour when Michelle stood up to stretch. "I don't know about you guys, but my back is screaming at me to stop."

Jack jumped up. "Mine too."

Beth laughed at her brother. "You're too young for your back to be hurting."

"Am not."

"You just want to go play a video game."

He dropped his bulb tool into the garden bucket and darted for the house. "Last one in is a rotten egg."

Michelle watched the kids race into the house. She went to put her tools in the bucket and noticed Jeff was still planting. She walked up behind him and kissed the back of his head. "It doesn't even look like you made a dent in that pile."

He chuckled. "I know."

She knelt down on the opposite side of the heart. "Why not lay a few of them where you want them so I can help you?"

"I thought you were finished for the night."

"Thought so too," she winked at him, "but someone has to rescue my handsome prince from this overwhelming pile."

He rubbed the back of his neck. She was right. It would take him forever to plant all of these. He picked up a bulb from the pile and gave it a small toss. "It might look like a never ending mountain, but come spring when they're all in bloom, you'll be in awe of how many days God has blessed us."

"I already am." Together they planted for another half hour. When the sunlight faded, they gathered everything up and put the tools in the shed for tomorrow. He placed his bucket of bulbs on the shelf by the door, then turned and pulled her into his arms. "You're worth every moment it takes for me to plant these."

Her arms went up around his neck and slowly he lowered his lips to hers. Their love entwined for a moment. There were no doubts, just the joy of two hearts beating as one.

They walked into the house arm in arm. It wasn't long before it was time for the kids to go to bed. Michelle said she was going too, because her head was throbbing. Jeff tossed up a silent prayer of thanks—not that Michelle had a headache, but that God was helping him with his plan.

He went into his office to do some work while waiting for everyone to fall asleep. A half hour later, he snuck up the stairs. At the door to their bedroom, he stood listening to Michelle's soft breathing. He whispered, "Sweet dreams," before quietly slipping back down the stairs.

On the way to the barn to get the hidden bulbs, he thought about Michelle's dream. When they'd first moved in, she talked about having the whole bank filled with tulips. One flower for every blessing. Ten years of blessings and there were many... but they still had a long way to go.

Smiling, he picked up a box of bulbs. *You will not die without seeing your dream. I promise.*

He got down on his hands and knees and started planting. He glanced up at the stars. "If I'm going to lose her, please let her hang on until Tulip of Love Day. Let her see this bank full of tulips. Please allow me to make her dream come true."

Every night after the rest of the family would go to sleep, Jeff sneaked out of the house and planted his tulips of love. On the third night, he was engrossed in the routine when a child's voice startled him.

"Dad, what are you doing out here?"

"Jack? Why aren't you in bed?"

"I heard you come down and thought you were getting a drink."

"You need to get back to bed."

"But, what are you doing?"

"I'm filling this bank with tulips."

"In the middle of the night?"

"It's a surprise for Mommy. You can't tell her."

Jack put his hands on his hips. "She isn't going to like that you just started planting bulbs without them standing for a blessing."

"Each one *is* for a blessing. There have been 191 days since we found out about the tumor. Twenty-four hours in each day, so... each one of these tulips represents one of those hours."

Jack grinned. "Can I help?"

Jeff handed him a bulb tool. "Just a little, then you need to get back to bed. You have school tomorrow."

They worked in silence. Together they made quick work of the pile Jeff had put out for that night. Suddenly Jack asked, "What if she dies before spring?"

Jeff put his tool down and pulled his son to him. "I'm not going to lie to you and say that won't happen, but we need to have faith that it won't. I know it's hard, but God has answered our prayers so far, and we can only hope He will continue to do so."

"I don't want her to die."

"Me either. But we really don't have a say in that, do we?"

Jack shook his head. "Hallelujah."

That one word took Jeff's breath away. "Hallelujah," he affirmed.

"Mommy loves that word, doesn't she?"

"Yes, she does."

"She says you can't say it without feeling it in your heart."

"I believe she's right." Jeff touched his heart. "Can't you feel the ray of love inside you when you say it?"

Jack put his hand on his heart and said, "Hallelujah." His face broke into a bright smile. "I can feel it."

"That's why Mommy loves that word. You cannot praise God and feel bad at the same time."

"Mommy says it's easy to praise God when things are going good, but to praise Him when life is falling apart takes courage." Jack picked up his tool and planted his next bulb. "We have courage, don't we?"

Jeff gave Jack a sideward hug. "We sure do."

After that, each night Jack would sneak out with his dad and together they covered the bank from one end to the other with tulips of every color. They talked in whispers about faith, baseball, football and whatever Jack had on his mind. They were co-conspirators on a mission to make Michelle's dream come true. When the last bulb went into the ground, they high-fived each other.

"Mommy is going to be so surprised," Jack said.

Jeff put his arm around Jack's shoulders. "Our secret."

"I bet she cries."

"I bet you're right."

.

Chapter 17

The blinking lights from the Christmas tree right outside her office door were driving her insane. Michelle laid her head into her hands. The headache wasn't helping matters. She needed to get this design done so she could get out of here. She glared at the paper in front of her. It looked like a three year old had attacked her drawing... the lines were anything but straight.

She hurled her pencil across the room, balled the sketch, and sent it flying after the pencil. Shadow lifted his head and looked at her.

"What are you looking at?" Michelle said with gritted teeth before laying her head down on her desk. It took every ounce of strength to control the scream that was bursting to let loose.

Debbie walked by the open door. "Michelle!" she yelled and rushed into the office.

Michelle raised a hand, but not her head. She murmured, "Headache."

"Where are your pills?"

"Took one already. Just need to rest a few minutes before I can go home."

"What can I get you?" Debbie hovered over her. "Tea, water?"

Michelle felt her hands tighten into fists. *Just leave me alone,* she screamed to herself. Gritting her teeth she whispered, "Quiet." Relief filled her when Debbie turned out the lights and shut the door.

She groaned when a few minutes later Nicole peeked in. "Do you want me to take you home?"

Michelle tried to raise her head again, but the movement caused a flash of lightning to pierce her brain. She moaned and managed to say, "Fifteen minutes."

Nicole backed out of the office and closed the door as softly as possible.

It was half an hour before the pills worked enough to allow her to lift her head and manage the short ride home.

Nicole helped her into the guest room and got her a drink of water. "You sure you don't want me to stay?"

"No."

"Should I call Jeff?"

Michelle looked to see where the dog had gone. He was not in the room, which meant she wasn't having a seizure, just a mental breakdown. *Small comfort.* She pulled the covers over her eyes and said, "I just need to sleep."

"I'll bring the kids home later and if you aren't better, I'll hang out with them until Jeff gets back."

Michelle's whole body went rigid. It took every ounce of self-control not to scream, *Leave me alone!* Somehow she managed to say, "Thanks."

When the front door shut, she breathed a sigh of relief and fell asleep. When she woke, her head didn't feel as bad. She looked at the clock beside the bed. An hour had passed and the kids would soon be home. She started to sit up, but the move made her nauseous. She laid back down.

Twenty minutes later, the door opened and the kids rushed in. She could hear Nicole trying to hush them. Michelle sat up and this time she felt better. She went into the hallway to greet the kids.

"How are you feeling?" Nicole asked.

"Much better."

"Do you need me to stay?"

"No, we'll be fine. It's just a dull ache now." She rubbed her head. "I can handle that." Michelle hugged Beth then Jack. "How was your day?"

They both started talking at once. "Please, one at a time," Michelle snapped.

Beth clamped her mouth shut.

Jack just kept right on talking. "Everyone loved the cookies you made for our party today." He put the empty container on the island. "The silly girls didn't want to eat them they were so pretty." He rushed over to the cookie jar and grabbed another one. "Not me." He stuffed the cookie into his mouth, icing covering his lips.

"Jack." Michelle closed her eyes and counted to three.

"Mom, why isn't the tree on?" Beth rushed into the family room. "Can I turn on the Christmas lights?"

"Yes, just don't make them blink."

The kids flopped down on the sofa. Michelle grabbed a bag of potatoes from the pantry.

"I'm not watching that girl cartoon." Jack grabbed the remote from Beth.

"Well, I'm not watching your stupid stuff." Beth ripped the remote out of Jack's hand and changed back to her show. Jack tried to steal the controller again.

"Pick something or I'm turning it off," Michelle barked. She pointed the potato peeler at them. "Figure it out or go to your rooms." Peelings started flying all over the counter as she attacked the potato in her hand.

A few minutes later, Beth complained, "He's touching me."

"Why don't you go outside and play?"

Jack jumped up from the sofa. "It's snowing."

Beth had to grab his drink before it spilled.

Michelle glanced out the window. Soft flakes were just beginning to fall. *Great. Just what we needed, a snowstorm.* She rubbed her head. What was wrong with her? She loved snow. But today it only irritated her. She closed her eyes. Everything irritated her today.

"It's going to be a white Christmas," Beth announced, clapping her hands.

"Go get your boots and coats on. We should feed the horses before it really starts coming down."

Jack and Shadow were the first to dash out the door. Shadow leaped up nipping at the snowflakes. Jack took off, slip-sliding across the wet patio. "Woohoo." He laughed as he landed face first into the snow.

"Jack, get up." Michelle hurried toward the barn. "You check the water, and Beth, you get the grain while I get the hay." Her horse Mandy came trotting up to her. "No treat today, girl." Michelle pushed the mare away.

Mandy followed her into the barn, nuzzling her arm.

"Go away," Michelle snapped. The horse looked at her. Michelle took a deep breath. "Sorry, girl." She put her arms around Mandy's neck and laid her head against the mane. *What's wrong with me?*

Once the horses and the barn cats were fed, they hurried toward the house. The snow was already accumulating.

"Can we play in the snow?"

"For a little bit," Michelle answered, and closed the mudroom door behind her.

She watched them run around the yard. When Beth laid down to make a snow angel, Michelle almost yelled for her not to get all wet. Instead, she turned away, wondering once again what was wrong with her. She would normally be out there making snow angels with the children. But she'd been on edge all day, feeling like she was a second away from exploding.

She went back to peeling the potatoes, attacking them as if they were the enemy. Peels flew everywhere. After she put them in a pot and placed the chicken in the oven, she called the kids to come in.

"Why do we have to come in now?" Jack complained. "We were having fun."

"It's getting dark, and it's cold outside."

"But—"

"No buts. I said come in. And I mean now."

Jack stormed into the house mumbling under his breath. He tracked snow across the family room and Shadow shook himself off, sending water everywhere.

"Get that dog out of the family room. Now."

Jack looked wide-eyed at his mother.

She pointed her finger at him. "Why didn't you come in through the mudroom like Beth did?" She grabbed a towel from the laundry room and tossed it at him. "Now clean that mess up." She stared at him staring at her. "Now."

She spun around and went back to finishing up dinner. She gripped the side of the countertop. "Your father will be here any minute, so please set the table."

Beth grabbed the plates and Jack the silverware. "You're doing it wrong," Beth scolded her brother.

"I'm not." They started pushing each other.

"*Stop!*" Michelle screamed. With a sweep of her hand, the salad bowl went flying off the counter, crashing onto the floor. She grabbed her head. "Just stop."

The kids froze. The shocked look on their faces was Michelle's undoing.

"What's going on?" Jeff said, rushing into the kitchen just as Michelle collapsed to the floor in tears.

"I'm sorry. I'm sorry," she whispered over and over.

Jeff ran to her. He tried to help her up but she pushed him away.

Her body racked with uncontrollable sobs. "I can't take this."

Jeff sat down on the floor beside her and rubbed her back. "It's going to be okay."

She glanced sideways at him. "Is it?" She pushed his hand off of her. "All day I have felt this rage building in me." He reached for her hand, but she scooted away. "Don't touch me."

The hurt in his eyes tore through her faster than any pain. "The doctor warned us this could happen." She looked at the salad and broken dish all over the floor. "What if this is who I'm becoming?" She flicked a piece of lettuce away from her. "An angry, hateful person." She crawled over to the broken bowl and started to pick it up. She looked toward the ceiling and said, "If this is what I'm turning into, then God, let me die now."

"NOOOOOOOOOOOO!" Jack and Beth screamed at once and ran to her, throwing their arms around her. "We're sorry. We didn't mean to make you mad."

Still on the floor, Michelle pulled the children onto her lap. "It's not your fault. I'm the one that's sorry."

Jeff wrapped them all in his arms. "I think this calls for our special word."

Together Jeff and the kids said, "Hallelujah."

"Michelle..." Jeff coached, "...Say your word."

Begrudgingly she said, "Hallelujah."

"Like you mean it."

Michelle glared at him. "Hallelujah," she said again, this time with more feeling. One more hallelujah and she started to smile. Finally, she lifted her hands to the air before bowing her head to pray. "Lord, please forgive my outburst. I don't know what came over me, but this is not who I am. Please put your healing hands on my head and take this burden from me." She wiped the tears from her face and kissed the cheeks of her family. "I need to clean this mess up."

"We'll help," Beth said.

"No, there's broken glass all over here. You two finish setting the table."

Michelle tried to join in the dinner conversation, but her heart wasn't in it. The anger was gone now, but she felt so disconnected from her family, from God, and from herself. The food tasted like sawdust. Her head throbbed, but it was nothing compared to the emptiness she felt in her heart. She just wanted to cry.

When dinner was over, she started to clear the table. "We got this," Jeff said. "Why don't you go relax?" Normally the four of them made quick work of the cleanup, but tonight she took him up on his offer.

"I do need to wrap some presents." She went into the office and shut the door. The pile of bags filled with gifts still needing to be wrapped only lured the anger out of hiding. Tomorrow was Christmas Eve and she still had too much to do.

Michelle sank down on the floor, putting her head to her knees. *Please God, I can't do this.* She grabbed the first bag from the pile and ripped it open, tossing it on the floor in front of her. *Calm down, this will get you nowhere.* Taking a deep breath she softly whispered, "Hallelujah."

It only took a moment for the calm to return, so she picked up the contents of the bag—a sweater for Jeff's mother, a blouse for Debbie, and a purse for Annette. She put the tops in one pile and the purse in another, before emptying a second bag. She dumped out five bags altogether, sorting them into neat stacks—one that could go in boxes, and the other which would need to be wrapped.

There was a knock on the door. Jeff peeked in. "Can I come in?"

"Yes."

He handed her a cup of tea.

"My tulip cup." She couldn't help but smile.

"It's a shame to only use it once a year, when you love it so much."

She took a sip. "Thank you."

He sat down beside her. "Need help?"

"Sure." She glanced at the door. "What are the kids doing?"

"Watching *Rudolph*."

She pointed to a pile. "That bunch just needs to be put into gift boxes."

He grinned. "Don't trust me with the wrapping paper, huh?"

"I've seen your wrap job. The boxes are safer for you."

"*Hmph.*"

She giggled. For the first time today she didn't feel like screaming. He picked up the flannel shirt on the top of the stack and placed it directly in a box.

"You need to put tissue paper in it first," she said, pointing to the folded stack in a variety of colors, then she handed him a tag. "That shirt is for your father."

Together they tackled the two stacks. Jeff picked up a bright orange and green flowered blouse. "Debbie?"

"How did you guess?"

"Looks like the gaudy stuff she wears."

"Her style is different, but it looks good on her."

"You actually like this?"

"It's pretty."

He rubbed his eyes and looked at it again. Then he looked back at her and shook his head. "Do me a favor and don't ever wear something like this."

"It's not my style."

"Hallelujah."

She tilted her head back and laughed.

"There it is."

Between the giggles she managed to ask, "What?"

"Your beautiful smile." He laid his hand over his heart. "Every time I see it, it makes me fall in love with you all over again."

"You're silly."

"It's true. Every day I look forward to walking into the house and being greeted by that gorgeous smile."

She lowered her head. "Sorry it wasn't there today."

"Do you want to talk about what happened?"

She shook her head and gave a big sigh. "Not really."

Jeff lifted her chin, forcing her to look at him. "How can I help if I don't know what's going on?"

"Honestly, I'm not sure what happened." She felt tears stinging her eyes. "All I know is all day I have felt like I was about to lose control... and then I did."

"Debbie said you had a really bad headache."

"Debbie is a big tattletale."

"She worries about you."

"I know."

Jeff reached over and lifted her onto his lap. She laid her head on his shoulder. "How's the headache now?" he asked.

"Manageable." She played with a button on his shirt. "Things are starting to get worse."

"I know."

She buried her face into his chest. "I was serious about what I said earlier."

"What?"

"I will pray to die, if this is who I'm going to become."

He lifted her face with his finger, looking her in the eyes again, and said, "No, Michelle, you will not."

"I can't."

"God is in control, and He will control this."

"Jeff, what if I die tonight and the last thing the kids remember about me is how angry I was? I flung the salad across the room. I can't be that person."

"And you aren't."

"But today I was."

"Then we add that to our prayer."

She whispered, "I'm scared."

"And what do we say when we are scared?"

Michelle buried her face into his chest and whispered, "Hallelujah."

He kissed the top of her head and repeated, "Hallelujah." Then they hugged each other tight. "You want to pray?" he asked.

"Yes."

They bowed their heads and prayed for strength to get through whatever lay ahead.

Michelle timidly smiled. "This wrapping can wait until later. Let's go finish watching *Rudolph* with the kids."

Jeff took her hand and pulled her up from the carpet. "Great idea."

Beth and Jack laid on the floor in front of the TV. Big smiles brightened their faces when they saw their parents coming. Michelle sat down on the sofa, so both kids climbed up and cuddled in beside her. She kissed the top of their heads and whispered, "I love you."

"Love you, too," they both replied.

The Christmas tree lights were glaring in her eyes. She could feel the headache return. She closed her eyes and said a fast prayer asking for relief. She was glad when *Rudolph* finished. "Who wants hot chocolate?"

Everyone raised their hands.

She clicked off the TV and said, "While I make it, why don't the three of you go into the dining room and work on wrapping the gifts you have for your cousins and grandparents?"

Jeff grinned. "You're going to trust me to help them?"

She snickered and said, "Okay, maybe you had better wait."

"I'm a good wrapper," Beth said.

"Yes, you are. So why don't you help the guys until I get in there?"

"Can we listen to Christmas music?" Jack asked.

"Of course," Jeff said. "Alexa, play Christmas music." Jingle Bells filled the room.

Beth and Jack put their bags of presents on the dining room table. Jeff pulled the container of wrapping paper up next to them. They were well on their way when Michelle brought in the hot chocolate and cookies.

Beth picked up the box of Wockenfuss candy for her grandmother. "Remember last year when Jack wrapped NaNa's chocolate, but put Pop-pop's name on it and then he refused to give it to her?" Beth snickered.

Jack smacked his forehead. "I won't do that again."

"I think you should." Jeff grinned. "Why not give her Pop-pop's gift pack of nuts?"

Jack clapped his hands with glee. He looked at Michelle and asked, "Can I, Mom?"

"They're your dad's parents, so it's totally up to him."

"Do it," Beth said. "It will be so funny when she opens it."

"But make sure she still gets her candy," Michelle said. "We don't want her cheated two years in a row." Excited voices rose around her. Relief filled her as, instead of anger, her heart felt happy. She glanced around at her family, soaking in the memory of this moment.

She took a deep breath. *What a difference a few hours made.* She closed her eyes and said a quick prayer. *Thank you for calming the rage within me and giving my family this time of laughter. Please don't let it end.*

Chapter 18

"Merry Christmas!" Beth and Jack leaped onto their parents' bed and Michelle jolted awake. The sudden movement caused the room to spin. She threw a hand over her mouth and made a dash to the bathroom. A flash of exploding pain knocked her to the floor.

"Michelle." Jeff's voice sound garbled and so far away.

She gagged trying to hold the vomit in. She felt herself being lifted off the floor, before being eased down beside the toilet just in time. Jeff held her hair away from her face, and rubbed her back. When she was finished, she collapsed onto the tile.

His arms went under her as if to lift her again.

"No, let me lie here a few minutes," she barely managed to whisper.

Her husband turned and saw the kids huddled together, eyes brimming.

"We d-d-didn't mean to m-m-make her sick..." Beth's voice shook with anguish.

Jeff joined them on the bed, pulling them into his arms. "You didn't cause this. Unfortunately, she wakes up with a bad headache many mornings. I'm going to get

Mommy a pill. The two of you go back to your rooms and I will come get you once her headache is gone."

"Okay." They both glanced at the bathroom door... their excitement from a few moments ago was replaced with fear.

Jeff rushed back into the bathroom. "Do you think you can take a pill without throwing up?"

Michelle mumbled, "If I don't move."

He helped her sit up slightly and handed her a glass of water and the tablet. She took it and laid back down.

"Want me to carry you back to bed now?"

"No, the cold floor feels good on my head."

He laid down beside her and rubbed her back. About fifteen minutes later she sat up. "I'm feeling a little better." He started to slide his hands underneath her, but she stopped him. "No. I can walk."

"And I can carry you." He swooped her up with ease, and laid her gently down on the bed, pulling the covers up around her shoulders. "Close your eyes." He kissed her cheek and added, "I'll keep the kids quiet."

"I do need to rest here a bit," she said. "Why don't you get the kids and we can read the birth of Jesus in here?"

"You sure?"

"It's our tradition. I can listen just as well laying here as sitting up."

Jeff brought Beth and Jack back into the bedroom. He pulled the cushion bench from the foot of the bed, around to Michelle's side. "The three of us are going to sit here, so we don't jar the bed."

"I'm better now, you can climb in with me." She patted the comforter.

Jeff leaned over and kissed her forehead. "We are good right here. You just close your eyes and listen to the miracle of Jesus' birth." Beth and Jack cuddled beside him.

Jeff turned to Luke, chapter 2. "...*But Mary treasured up all these things and pondered them in her heart. The shepherds returned, glorifying and praising God for all the things they had heard and seen which were just as they had been told.*"

When Jeff read the final word, Michelle felt the pain subside. She sat up smiling. "Wow, look at that sunrise." She slipped out of bed and padded over to the French doors leading to the balcony. A blast of cold air filled the room as she stepped out.

Jeff grabbed a blanket from the bed before following her. He draped it around her shoulders and pulled the kids in front of them to snuggle everyone close.

"I love when God paints the sky with shades of orange," Michelle whispered in awe. "What a beautiful gift God has given us to start this glorious day."

Suddenly Beth started to sing, "O Little Town of Bethlehem," and the others joined in. Michelle's heart swelled with joy. She raised her hands up and shouted, "Hallelujah."

Downstairs, Michelle put the teakettle on before placing the breakfast casserole in the oven. Jeff and the kids were still upstairs. She turned on the Christmas tree lights and called for her family to come join her.

The kids would normally race down, fighting for the right to be the first to see what Santa had brought, only this morning there was a touch of solemnness about them. Michelle wished she could rewind time and not have them see her as they had this morning. Though they were smiling, she could feel their fear that this would be their last Christmas together.

Christmas day passed in a whirlwind of presents, family and food. Her headache never returned.

A few days later, Jeff woke up and was surprised to see Michelle still asleep. He laid his hand lightly on her back to make sure she was breathing. She gave a slight moan. He exhaled a sigh of relief. "Thank you, God, for another day."

He gently rolled out of bed, pulled on a pair of jeans, and went downstairs to start breakfast, his normal Sunday breakfast.

The kids soon joined him. "Where's Mom?"

"Still sleeping."

"Is she okay?" Beth cautiously asked.

"Yes, she just needs some extra sleep." Jeff looked into the refrigerator. "What do you think I should put in the pancakes this morning?" He pulled out some leftover turkey.

"*No.*" Jack put his hand out in front of him. He peeked around his father at all the food. "Can't we just have normal pancakes? Like with chocolate chips," Jack said.

"Yeah, chocolate chips."

Jeff grabbed the package of blueberries. "I think we have all had enough sweets the last couple of days. It's time to eat healthy."

"Who are you and what did you do with my husband?"

Jeff spun around, grinning. "Sleeping beauty, you decided to join us." He winked.

"Why didn't you wake me?" Michelle asked.

"Figured you needed the rest." He went to the stove and poured her a cup of tea. "I kept the water hot for you."

She took the cup with her left hand, splashing some hot water as she set it on the counter. He watched as she awkwardly added honey, again using the wrong hand.

"Michelle..." He glanced at her right arm, tucked inside the pocket of her jeans. "What's going on?"

"Arm is asleep, that's all."

He came around the counter and started rubbing the limp arm. "Does that make it feel better?"

She lowered her eyes and said, "A little." She nodded toward the stove. "I think the pancakes are done."

Jeff rushed to the stove, rescuing the pancakes before they burned. "*Phew*, that was a close one." He flipped the last ones onto a platter and carried them to the table. The kids filled their plates.

Jack shoved a piece of bacon into his mouth. "I love bacon."

"You say that every time," Beth said, reaching for a piece.

"How do you think I would look with short hair?" Michelle cautiously asked.

Beth dropped her bacon and stared at her mother.

"What kind of question is that?" Jeff said.

"I'm thinking it's about time I cut it."

Beth jumped up from her seat and raced around the table, throwing her arms around her mother. "No, Mommy, no."

Jeff looked at her. "Why? You love your long hair."

"It will be easier to take care of if it's short."

"Are you having problems now?" Jeff questioned.

She shrugged her shoulders.

"Michelle?"

She glanced down at her arm. "My right arm is numb, and the left one's really shaky." Her voice quivered. "Look at my hair... I couldn't even brush it today."

Beth rushed out of the room. They could hear her running up the stairs. A few moments later she returned carrying Michelle's brush. "I can brush your hair, Mommy," Beth said. "And fix it the way you like it. You know I can."

"I can help, too," Jack said.

"There, that's settled," Jeff said. "No haircuts."

Michelle shook her head. "For now."

They sat down to eat. Michelle tried to cut her pancakes with her left hand, but was having trouble. Beth got up, walked around the table to her mother's side, and sliced the food into bite-sized pieces.

Michelle's eyes teared up. "Thank you."

Beth hugged her and said, "You're welcome," before sitting back down to finish her own breakfast.

Michelle only picked at her food. Eventually she pushed back her chair, holding her stomach. "I need to lie down."

Jeff followed her into the hallway. "You okay?"

She shook her head. "Both arms are tingling now and I feel sick to my stomach."

He helped her up the stairs, one step at a time, and tucked her into bed. "I'm going to call your parents to come and get the kids for church."

"You don't have to stay home with me."

"I'm not leaving you alone." He picked up his cell and called her mother. Hanging up, he said, "They'll be here in twenty, so I better get the kids ready."

When he came back in, Michelle was in the bathroom with the door closed. He sat down on the edge of the bed and waited for her to come out. After a few minutes, he knocked on the door. "You okay?"

He heard a soft sob.

"I'm coming in." He slowly turned the knob, cautiously peeking in.

"Jeff, I'm on the toilet," she gasped in dismay.

"I see that." He wiped tears from her face. "What's going on?" he asked.

She looked at her hands laying on her lap. "Both arms are numb, I can't pull up my pants, or..." she hung her head, "or wipe."

Jeff pulled some toilet paper from the roll.

"What are you doing?" Her eyes grew wide in horror.

"I'm going to wipe you," he answered.

"No." Her bottom lip trembled.

"Why not?"

She hung her head. "It's disgusting."

He knelt down in front of her. "Look at me." When he held her eyes with his he said, "There is nothing disgusting about you."

She lowered her eyes. "What if I had—"

"Nothing."

"This is so humiliating." A sob caught in her throat.

"Nah."

She stared over his shoulder as he lifted her slightly and reached around to wipe. "This is my job as your husband, to take care of whatever need you have. If that means wiping you, dressing you, or..." He got a big grin, "...or bathing you, then I'll do it." He helped her stand from the toilet and then pulled her pants up.

"I need to wash my hands," Michelle said.

"But you didn't wipe."

"I still need to wash them."

Jeff turned on the water, then squirted soap into his palm and washed their hands together. He glanced at Michelle's eyes in the mirror. A mixture of fear and hopelessness looked back at him. He kissed her cheek. "You know there is nothing I wouldn't do for you."

She nodded.

"I'm going to call the doctor and tell him what's going on."

"That isn't necessary. The last time my arm went numb—"

"This happened before?"

"The other day..."

"Why didn't you tell me?"

"It was only for a half hour. Honestly, I just thought my arm went to sleep."

He walked her to the bed. "Your parents will be here to get the kids soon. Then I'm calling the doctor." He covered her up. "Try and get some sleep."

She sighed.

Jeff quietly closed the door. He lifted his eyes upward. *Is this a sign You are not going to heal her?* He clenched his hands to his chest. *Please, God—*

The doorbell rang, then Kay walked in. She glanced up the stairs at Jeff. Panic filled her eyes.

"Is she—"

"She's just having a bad day," he said, coming down to greet her. "She'll be fine." Then he glanced upward and silently added, *Please.*

Chapter 19

The doctor ordered Michelle to go to the ER immediately. The staff was expecting her and took her straight back for an MRI.

Shortly afterward, Dr. Carson came into the room. He patted her hand and looked apologetically at Jeff. "This is the day we have been dreading. For the last ten months, there has been little to no change in the tumor. Unfortunately, we can no longer say that."

"What does that mean?" Jeff asked.

"I'm sorry to say the tumor has grown."

Michelle nodded.

Jeff sank down into the chair beside her bed. "So, what can we do about it?"

"Nothing."

"We can pray." Jeff placed Michelle's hand in his.

The doctor shook his head.

"Don't you believe in prayer?" Michelle asked.

"I believe in facts."

"You do believe in Jesus, don't you?"

"Not the way you do."

"Then we will pray for you, too."

The doctor gave her a condescending smile. "I'm going to have the nurse give you a shot of morphine."

"No," Michelle said adamantly.

"It will help the pain."

"God is helping me deal with the pain."

Dr. Carson stared at her for a moment. "It's your choice, but I think it's best if we admit you."

"Why? You said there was nothing you could do."

"We can make you comfortable."

"But I'm not going to take your drugs."

"You might change your mind."

"How long?" Jeff whispered.

"Anytime."

"Then I'm taking her home."

"I wouldn't advise it."

"She's my wife and I will take care of her."

Dr. Carson looked at Michelle. "You will need twenty-four hour care." She nodded. Then he glanced at Jeff and said, "I don't think you understand what you're signing up for."

"I signed up for life, good or bad." Jeff squeezed Michelle's hand. "I fully understand."

"You do realize that she can't even feed or dress herself."

"I have undressed her for years."

"Jeff," Michelle gasped. She felt heat rise in her face. "Really?"

He winked at her. "I'm sure I can figure out how to put her clothes back on." Michelle glared at him.

"I'm sure you can," Dr. Carson said, "but things are just going to get worse."

"I understand that. And if anyone is going to take care of her, it will be me."

"Michelle," Dr. Carson patted her hand. "What do you want?"

She looked around her. Machines were beeping, doctors and nurses were rushing past her door. She could hear someone crying, and another person moaning in pain. "I want to go home."

"Are you sure?"

"Yes."

"We will be better able to take care of you when the time—"

She interrupted him. "I will get better at home."

"Michelle—"

She turned her head toward Jeff and asked, "Will you get me ready?"

Dr. Carson left shaking his head. "The nurse will be in shortly with your discharge papers."

Jeff helped Michelle into their SUV and buckled her seatbelt, then settled her hands on her lap. He gave her a quick kiss, before shutting the door. Michelle stared out of the car window as he pulled from the parking lot.

Jeff reached over and took her hand in his. "We have been on this ride before."

She nodded.

"It's been ten months and nothing really has changed."

"How can you say that?" She looked down at her hands. "I can't even move my arms."

"The diagnosis is the same, and I still believe God will give us our miracle."

"What if He doesn't?"

"He will."

She sighed. "I want to believe with my whole heart and soul that God will heal me."

"Then He will."

She looked at him. "Jeff, I am getting worse, not better. You have to be prepared for the worst."

Her husband pulled into their driveway and stopped. He reached over and pulled her to him. "Until you take your last breath, I will continue to believe God will grant us the miracle."

"And if He doesn't, what will that do to your faith?"

"You mean, will I be angry with God if you... die?" His voice broke on the word. "I won't lie and say no. But as you are so fond of saying, God is big enough to take our anger. I know that no matter what the outcome is, God is still God, and nothing can change that. If He doesn't heal you, I will deal with it then, but not before." He rested his forehead on hers. "Don't worry. I will not lose my faith. How else will I be able to join you in heaven?" He kissed her. "Now, no more talk about dying. Until your last breath, we talk about your living."

She rested her head on his shoulder.

"I have a question," Jeff said, caressing her back. "The doctor said he didn't understand how you were tolerating the pain without stronger meds. How bad is it?"

"Pretty bad."

"How are you dealing with it?"

She shrugged her shoulders. "The pain I can handle. The problem is the anger."

"But you haven't been angry since that day..."

Michelle shook her head. "I wish that was true."

"Well, you don't seem angry."

She snickered. "That's because every time I feel the rage building I run out to the greenhouse and scream to God to take it away."

"Is that why there's so much basil in the fridge?"

She grinned. "Yes."

"Then it must help."

"It does."

"The kids and I will try and do better at not irritating you."

"Honestly, there's nothing you can do. When I feel the rage, everything makes me mad."

"Michelle!" Jeff shouted. "You just squeezed my hand."

"I did?" She looked down at her lap. She attempted to move both sets of fingers and was surprised when the left hand moved. "Hallelujah," she laughed.

Jeff jumped out of the vehicle, raced to her side of the car and opened her door. Before she could step out, he scooped her up laughing. He shouted to the sky, "Thank you, Lord, for this answer to our prayers."

The next morning, the numbness in Michelle's arms was gone. Each step she took to the bathroom, she sang hallelujah to herself. She dressed and went downstairs, pushed the button to start Jeff's coffee, turned on the teapot, then headed out to the sunroom to read her Bible.

Her heart filled with joy as she watched the sun slowly creep over the hill. This time in the morning—

when the house was quiet and nature was just about to wake—was the time she felt closest to God.

She opened her Bible to read whatever page she turned to, as was her habit. This morning it was John 9:3, *"Jesus answered, Neither hath this man sinned, nor his parents: but that the works of God should be made manifest in him."*

Michelle bowed her head. *Are You trying to tell me something?* She felt a peace fill her. She remained in the sunroom enjoying her time with God until the kettle whistled.

After brewing her tea, she made biscuits and put them in the oven before starting to cook bacon. She smiled because once the aroma wafted up the stairs, it would only be a matter of time before the others would join her.

Jeff was the first one down. "What are you doing?"

She raised both arms. "Today is a good day."

He picked her up and spun her around. "Hallelujah."

"Put me down, you goof. The bacon is about to burn."

He set her down, kissed her sweetly on the lips, and said, "I love bacon almost as much as I love you."

"Glad I'm ahead of bacon."

"You are ahead of everything but God." He winked. "God, you, the kids..." While she was distracted, he reached out and grabbed a piece of bacon. "Then bacon."

Michelle tried to smack his hand, but he was too fast.

Jack came running into the kitchen yelling, "Bacon!" He also tried to grab a piece, but Michelle held the plate out of his reach.

Jeff sneaked up behind her, stole a piece from the top, and handed it to their son. "There you go, bud."

"Jeff." Michelle pretended to scold him, but couldn't keep from laughing. She pointed to the table. "Go sit down. Obviously you can't be trusted."

She took the biscuits out of the oven and finished cooking the eggs before sitting at the table with them. They bowed their heads and prayed over the food and the day. Both kids kissed her goodbye and ran out the door to the truck as Jeff kissed the top of her head and said, "I'm going to stop in the office for a few minutes, once I drop the kids off. Then I will be back."

She nodded. As she watched him leave, she felt a little agitated. Just yesterday he had vowed to take care of her, and not even a day later he was rushing off to work. Sure, she was fine right now, but what would happen if it didn't continue? She hit her head with her hands. *Just stop it*, she scolded herself.

Jeff called his brothers into the office and meanwhile had Debbie call out to the shop to request a meeting before everyone left for the day's jobs. After talking with his brothers, they joined the others in the conference room.

"Yesterday, Michelle took a turn for the worst," Jeff said. There was a collective gasp. He held his hand up.

"Today, she is fine." After a deep breath he continued, "The tumor has started to grow, and the doctor really doesn't think she has much time left."

Debbie put her hands over her face.

"But we aren't giving up hope. He told us the same thing ten months ago. With all our prayers she made it this far. I would ask that you all continue to pray for her healing. I know it is coming, we just don't know when. So, in the meantime, I have asked Bob and Jason to step in with the everyday running of the business. Bob will take over the Woodbine project and Jason on the Anderson's. I'm going to be staying with Michelle and taking care of her. I'm still only a phone call away."

He looked around the room. It wasn't only the women trying not to cry. Everyone loved Michelle. His heart swelled as he saw the grief on their faces.

"I will keep everyone informed on what's going on. Like I said... today is a good day. We can only pray it continues."

"Can we all p-pray for her n-now?" Debbie's voice cracked with unshed tears.

"Yes," others in the room said.

They all bowed their heads and prayed together for Michelle's healing.

Afterward, the men patted Jeff on the back and the women hugged him before leaving the room. The only ones left were his brothers and Debbie.

"What can we do to help?" she asked.

"Just keep praying. If we need anything I'll let you know."

"Can I call her?"

"Of course you can."

Debbie rushed from the room and went straight to the phone.

Jeff looked at his brothers. "And if you need me. Just call."

Jason rolled his eyes. "You know Mrs. Anderson hates me. I'm sure she'll be calling you as soon as I show up."

"She sees that baby face of yours and thinks you don't know what you're doing." Jeff jabbed Jason in the arm. "You just need to show her."

"If she lets me."

"She will." Jeff grabbed his coat. "She has no choice."

Before he even entered the kitchen from the garage, he could hear the mixer going. He pushed open the door. "What are you doing?"

"Making banana bread."

"Why?" He dropped his keys on the countertop. "Just yesterday you were in the hospital. Shouldn't you be resting?"

"Shouldn't you be at work?" She raised an eyebrow at him.

He walked up behind her and said, "I'm all yours." He put his arms around her waist.

"What about—"

"I told you I was going to take care of you."

Michelle waved her arms. "But there's no point. I'm fine today."

"The point is I love you. And that is the only point that matters." He kissed her cheek and brought her up to date. "Bob and Jason are taking over the running of the business. I'll handle the paperwork from home. It's all been settled."

"I hate causing all this trouble," Michelle groaned.

Jeff turned her around to face him. "You are never any trouble." Hugging her close he said, "This is what I signed up for when I married you. To be your partner, helper, lover and whatever else comes with the job."

"We can get a nurse like the doctor suggested."

He kissed the tip of her nose. "Nurse Jeff at your service."

She giggled. "Where's your nurse's hat?"

He matter of factly stated, "Oh, we don't wear them anymore."

"Too bad. I'm sure you would have looked so cute in one."

He nuzzled her neck. "You think I'm cute?"

"Nope."

"What?" He placed his hand over his heart.

"I think you're handsome."

"Why thank you, ma'am." He pretended to tip his hat at her.

She pushed him away. "Now let me finish this bread."

Jeff looked at the smashed banana in the food processor then over his shoulder at the counter. "You used those rotten bananas?"

"They weren't rotten, just ripe."

"I was going to compost them."

"Now you don't have to."

"Why would you use rotten..."

"They weren't rotten, and that's what I always use."

"Yuck."

"You love banana bread."

"That was before I knew you used rotten food."

She finished mixing the ingredients together. "Ripe bananas make the best bread and smoothies."

Jeff held his stomach. "Ugh, you're trying to kill us."

"Oh stop. It's delicious and you know it."

He put his finger in the batter and wiped it across her lips. Before she could clean it off, he kissed her. "Umm, rotten bananas taste good on you."

"You are a silly man." Michelle poured the batter in the loaf pans and carried two to the oven.

He followed her with the other two and asked, "Why so many?"

"I'm going to freeze two." She started to carry the dishes to the sink, but he took them from her.

"I'll do that."

"Don't you have some work to do?"

"It can wait. Right now, I want to help you."

"Fine. You rinse and I'll load them in the dishwasher." Together they made quick work of cleaning the kitchen.

"Now what do we do?"

"Relax until the bread comes out."

Jeff scooped her up into his arms. "I know how we can relax," he said with a wink.

"And not even five minutes ago you were worried about me making bread." She rolled her eyes at him. She kissed his cheek. "Put me down and go get some work done." When Jeff's cell phone rang, she said, "Saved by the bell."

He grimaced. "That didn't take long." He answered the call. "Mrs. Anderson, how nice to hear from you."

Michelle tried not to giggle. Jeff glared at her. On a good day, Mrs. Anderson was difficult. Jeff and his grandfather were the only ones who could make her happy.

"Jason is very capable of doing the job," he reassured, then walked out of the room and headed to his office. He was sure Michelle could hear him pacifying Mrs. Anderson all the way down the hall.

The bread was out of the oven before he returned. "Boy, do I feel sorry for her husband," he said.

Michelle looked up from sweeping the floor. "He isn't the most pleasant person either."

"I don't understand how they can live like that."

"That is why I pray for them."

"You pray for the Andersons?"

"Yes."

Jeff shook his head. "You are an amazing woman."

She only rolled her eyes. "So how did you calm her down?"

"I told her the truth. The second I told her about your tumor, she did a complete turnaround."

"You see... she does have compassion."

Jeff took the broom from her hands. "Well, I'm done talking about the Andersons. I want to talk about the Stevens."

"Oh really, what is there to talk about?"

He started to dance around the kitchen with her, eyeing the bread on the counter. "I'm ready for a nap, how about you?"

She placed the back of her arm to her forehead. "I do feel a little tired," she said in her best southern accent, then winked at him.

He grabbed her and carried her up the stairs. "I think I am going to like this nursing."

Chapter 20

Jeff woke to Shadow whining outside the door. He glanced at the clock; it was three A.M. He tried to ignore the dog, but Shadow was not giving up. Jeff opened the bedroom door. "Boy, it's too early to go out." Shadow rushed into their room straight to Michelle's side of the bed where he lay his head.

"She's okay, boy, she's sleeping."

Shadow refused to move.

"Alright," Jeff said and laid back down. "You can stay." What was with the dog? He usually never left Jack's side. Jeff sat up to look at Shadow. "What is it, boy?" He fluffed the pillow before laying back down.

He was just about to drift off when the bed started to shake. Jeff bolted upright. It took him a moment to realize Michelle was having a seizure.

"Michelle." He pulled the covers off her before gently rolling her onto her side. He closed his eyes and said a silent pray. *Please let me know how to help her.* The seizure lasted only a few minutes, but it felt like forever. Jeff rubbed her back until the shaking subsided.

She slept through the whole thing. It was the first one she'd had in weeks. He laid his head on her back. *Why, God? She'd had such a good day.*

When Shadow left the room, Jeff breathed a sigh of relief. He slept with his wife in his arms and every time she moved, he jerked awake.

At seven, he inched his way out of the bed, trying not to wake her. He was pulling on his jeans when Michelle started to sit up, but quickly fell back down. He walked to her side of the bed and sat next to her. After a blank stare, she closed her eyes.

"Go back to sleep."

Without opening her eyes, she said, "Okay."

That simple word told him today was not going to be a good day. There was no way she wouldn't have insisted on fixing breakfast if she had it together.

Jeff woke the kids before going to the kitchen to scramble eggs. After he dropped Beth and Jack off at the bus, he checked on Michelle again. She was still sleeping. He laid down beside her and quickly drifted off, too.

Suddenly, Michelle bolted upright. "Oh no, we overslept."

He grabbed her by the arm before she could jump out of bed. "No, we didn't," he said groggily.

"It's ten o'clock. The kids need to get to school."

"They're already there."

She gave him a puzzled look.

"I got them up and out the door," he explained.

"They went off without me saying I love you."

"They came in and kissed you goodbye. You said it to them."

She shook her head. "I don't remember."

Jeff put his arm around her. "You had a seizure last night."

"When?"

"In your sleep."

"Is that even possible?"

"I didn't think so, but yes, apparently it is."

"No wonder I feel so out of it."

"You should lay here a little while longer."

She laid back and closed her eyes. "Yeah."

Jeff stayed in bed until she fell back to sleep, then tiptoed out of the room and down the stairs to the office. It was noon before he heard her moving around. Dashing up the steps to check on her, he peeked in and asked, "You feeling better?"

"I can't believe I slept so long."

"You needed it."

"I guess."

"You hungry?"

"A little."

He turned to leave. "While you get dressed, I'll fix you something."

When she came down, he had made grilled cheese and tomato soup. He had the hot tea waiting on the table for her as well.

She smiled at him and said, "I could get used to this."

He kissed the top of her head before sitting down beside her.

The rest of the day sped by. Before they knew it, it was time to get the kids from the bus. They came bursting though the garage door, dropping their bookbags on the floor.

"Is that where they belong?" Jeff asked, following them in. They sheepishly grinned before picking them up and hanging them on the hooks by the door. They put their lunch boxes on the counter beside the sink, and went to their mother and hugged her.

"Are you feeling better?" Beth asked.

"Much better." Michelle kissed the top of her children's heads. "It's a nice day. Why don't you two go out and play for a while?"

Jack grabbed a cookie from the cookie jar before dashing outside with the dog yapping at his heels.

Jeff leaned against the French doors, drinking a cup of coffee and watching his children play. There was just enough snow left for them to have a snowball fight. He chuckled. "Come watch this." When she joined him at the door, he winked at Michelle and said, "I'll be right back." He grabbed his coat, went out through the garage, and snuck around the side of the house. The kids didn't even see him coming until they both were hit with a snowball.

"Hey!" Jack spun toward his father. "No fair."

"Nothing's fair in a snowball fight," Jeff said laughing. Snowballs flew from all directions. Laughter filled the air.

Michelle slowly walked to the edge of the patio. She waved a scarf and called, "Time out. We need to feed the horses."

Jeff heaved one last snowball in her direction. She jumped just in time to avoid being hit. "Don't you know the meaning of a waved flag?"

"It's not white." He laughed and the snowball fight continued, this time with Michelle ganging up with Beth against the boys.

A half hour later, Michelle succeeded in calling a truce. "Let's get the horses fed."

Once they were finished feeding the animals, she headed toward the house. "I'll start dinner while you guys play."

Jeff followed her to the kitchen. "Tell me what you want for dinner and I will fix it."

Michelle opened the pantry, reaching for a jar of marinara sauce and a box of spaghetti. "You can get the chicken thighs from the refrigerator."

Jeff looked at the meat. "What do I do with it?"

She took it from him. "Nothing," she answered and gently shoved him toward the door. "Go play with the kids. I have this."

"But—"

"I'm fine. Go enjoy the rest of the evening before it gets too dark."

The week flew by. She had good days followed by bad. In the middle of the second week, her head felt like it would explode, and she could barely sit up without feeling sick to her stomach. Even laying on the sofa hurt, so she turned off the TV. Between the noise and her vision, she couldn't bear watching it.

The phone rang and she struggled to sit up, but was grateful when it only rang twice.

Jeff came into the room. "It's Dorothy Lay, she wants to know if she can bring us lunch tomorrow. I told her I wasn't sure if you would be up to it."

"Oh, tell her yes. I love Miss Dorothy."

Her husband relayed the message and then hung up the phone. "Are you sure you'll be up to it? You haven't been able to eat anything at all today."

"Even if I can't eat, it will be nice to visit with her." Michelle leaned her head on the back of the sofa. "You know that's her ministry."

"What?"

"She visits the members of the church when they aren't feeling well. She brings them lunch and visits with them. She is such a Godsend to so many."

"I didn't know that."

"Some of them have no family around, so she might be their only visitor. She also sends cards."

"What do you think she'll bring for lunch?"

"Doesn't matter. What matters is she's coming."

Michelle prayed that she would be well enough to enjoy Miss Dorothy's visit. "I think I need to go lie down."

"Good idea."

"I'll be in the guest room, so you don't have to keep running up the stairs to check on me."

He grinned. "I try to be quiet."

"You are. I'm just not always asleep." She stood up and fell back down. Jeff rushed to her side. "I'm okay, just a little wobbly."

He lifted her into his arms.

"I can walk," she insisted.

"And I can still carry you." He kissed the tip of her nose. "All part of my nurse duties."

She laid her head on his shoulder. "Don't think any other nurse would be carrying me around the house."

"I'm not any nurse."

"No, you aren't." She kissed his chest.

He put her down near the bed, pulled the covers back, and helped her in. As he tucked the covers around her, he said, "I'll be in the office if you need me."

Michelle closed her eyes.

When she woke, the headache was more manageable. She walked to the office door and Jeff looked up from his laptop.

"You feeling better?"

"Much." She smiled. "Have you had lunch yet?"

He glanced at his watch. "Wow, didn't realize it was so late." He started to get up. She waved him back down.

"You finish up here, and I'll make us something."

In the kitchen, she looked in the refrigerator and was happy to see leftover tomato soup. Grilled cheese and soup, the perfect lunch.

When Jeff came in, he walked over to the stove. "Yum... my favorite. You need any help?"

"You can pour the drinks."

He was whistling as he poured iced tea in two glasses. The noise grated on Michelle's nerves. As they ate, he just kept talking. She wanted to scream. She squeezed her eyes shut. *Why don't you take this anger from me?* She shook her fist at the heavens. *Why?*

Shadow came up to the table, looking at Jeff with eyes that said, "Where is my food?" She shooed him away.

The dog laid down and covered his eyes with his paws. It irritated Michelle so much she jumped up and ran out the door to the greenhouse. Covering her ears, she screamed as loud as she could, before falling to her knees, praying for God to remove the anger building inside of her.

She felt Jeff's arms go around her. He held her until she was ready to lift her head. Wiping the tears from her face she finally said, "I'm okay now."

"Does the screaming really help?"

She attempted to smile. "Actually, it does. It's like all the pressure comes out of my mouth."

"Well, that was some scream. It made my heart stop."

She glanced sideways at him. "I'm sorry."

"Nothing to be sorry for."

She stood up, taking his hand in hers. "Now you know why I come out here. I don't want to scare anyone."

He pulled her into his arms. "I thought you said you were feeling better."

"I was. The rage has nothing to do with the headache. It just happened without warning." She lay her head against his chest. "I h-hate it." Her voice broke. "I would rather have a thousand headaches than one ounce of the fury that builds in me."

"Let's pray together for God to free you from this."

The next morning, she woke up and her head barely ached at all. When Jeff took the kids to the bus, she mixed up ingredients for a coffee cake.

"What are you doing?" Jeff asked, coming in from the garage.

"Making dessert for when Miss Dorothy comes."

"Glad to see you're feeling good today."

"Me, too." She looked upward. "Thank you, God."

Jeff poured himself another cup of coffee. "I'll be in the office if you need me."

At noontime the doorbell rang. Michelle beat him to answer it. "Miss Dorothy, how good to see you."

Jeff took the bags of food from their visitor. Michelle linked her arm with Miss Dorothy's and guided her into the house.

"What a beautiful home you have."

Michelle beamed. "Jeff did an awesome job, didn't he?"

Miss Dorothy looked at Jeff in surprise. "You built this?"

"Not completely, I took an old farm house and remodeled it."

"I thought you just did new builds."

"I do both, but my love is restoring someone's old love."

Miss Dorothy walked into the kitchen. "Old love?" she asked with a sparkle in her eye.

Michelle grinned. "He's a romantic."

Jeff laughed. "I guess I am. Old houses were once filled with love, and I hate to see them torn down." He placed the bags on the table.

Miss Dorothy started to unpack. "I stopped at Bullock's and got us chicken and macaroni salad. I hope that's okay," she said, placing the food on the table.

"Oh, we love Bullock's," Michelle said.

Miss Dorothy pulled out a pie. "I couldn't resist the apple pie."

Jeff rubbed his stomach. "Mmm."

Michelle pulled out a chair and said, "You sit here." She gave Miss Dorothy a quick hug, "I am so happy you came to visit."

Michelle smiled to herself as she watched Jeff push the coffee cake into the corner so it would be hidden by the refrigerator. "We have iced tea, lemonade, and water... or would you prefer coffee or hot tea?"

Michelle put out plates and silverware while Jeff filled the glasses.

"Water is fine."

After they blessed the food, Michelle passed the chicken around. For a few minutes, no one spoke. They just enjoyed their meal.

Miss Dorothy put her fork down. "Tell me, how are you doing?"

Michelle lowered her eyes and answered, "Fine."

Miss Dorothy laid her hand on Michelle's arm. "The truth."

"Other than the rage, I'm really doing okay."

"Rage?"

"One of the side effects of the tumor." Michelle played with the food on her plate. "It just happens and there's nothing I can do to stop it, other than screaming as loud as I can."

Jeff frowned. "It seems to help."

"When you first feel this rage, do you pray?"

Michelle stared wide-eyed at her. "Honestly, no. After I scream, I fall down on my knees and pray."

"Don't you think it's the prayer, and not the screaming that removes the anger?" Miss Dorothy asked.

"You're right." Michelle covered her face with her hand. "The anger is all I can think about."

"Do you remember the verse in Philippians about being anxious?"

"Not sure."

Jeff got up and went into the family room for his Bible. "Philippians what?"

"Chapter 4."

Jeff read aloud: "*Do not be anxious about anything, but in everything by prayer and supplication with thanksgiving let your requests be made known to God. And the peace of God, which surpasses all understanding, will guard your hearts and your minds in Christ Jesus.*"

Michelle stood, throwing her arms around Miss Dorothy's neck. "Thank you. Next time I feel the rage coming, I will definitely claim that verse." She sat back down. Before picking up her chicken she added, "You aren't just a Sunday School teacher, you are truly a gardener in God's garden."

Miss Dorothy laughed. "I don't know about that."

"I do." Michelle wiped her hands, then reached over and patted Miss Dorothy's arm. "Do you remember the first time I met you?"

"I know it was a long, long time ago."

"I was six years old and we'd just moved here from Baltimore. It was my first day at Sunday School in our new church and I was terrified. Annette, being a year younger than me, was going to be in a different class and I was not happy. But then I walked—more like I was pushed—by my mother into your classroom. When you saw me, you smiled. I will never forgot how happy you looked to see me, and then I wasn't afraid anymore."

"That was so long ago."

"Who would have thought that six year old would grow up to call you her friend?"

Miss Dorothy squeezed Michelle's hand. "It is my pleasure to be your friend."

"Before you, I don't remember any of my Sunday School teachers. I credit you for planting the first seeds of Jesus' love in my heart."

They talked some more, ate pie, and then Miss Dorothy left, promising to come back again. Jeff grabbed the coffee cake from the counter, putting it on the table in front of her. "No sense wasting a good dessert."

Michelle picked up her fork and tapped it against his. "Here's to double desserts and extra sweet husbands."

Chapter 21

Jeff didn't know how he knew. Maybe it was the change in her breathing, but he was aware the second she woke up. He said a silent prayer of thanks for giving him another day with his wife. He noticed her inching her way to the edge of the bed, but barely felt the mattress give when she stood up. If he had been sleeping deeply—like he had for years—he never would have felt it.

Silently she tiptoed to the bathroom. He knew from watching her every morning she wouldn't turn the light on until after she had shut the door.

Jeff was asleep again before she left the bathroom.

"*Aaaaaaah!*" Her scream jolted him awake. *Thump, thump, thump* . Panic flooded through him as he leaped out of bed and flew to the stairs. His heart stopped at the sight of his wife's crumpled body lying at the bottom of the steps.

Within seconds, he was by her side. "Michelle." He touched her face and thankfully, her eyes fluttered open. "Thank you, God, she's alive."

She tried to move.

"Don't move," he coached.

"Mommy!" Beth and Jack cried at once.

Jeff looked up at the top of the stairs. The children stood clinging together.

"She's going to be okay," he said with a confidence he didn't feel. Quickly he checked to see if anything was broken.

Shadow pushed his way past Jeff and jumped over Michelle, laying beside her whimpering.

"What hurts?" he asked.

"Ev-ry-th-g." She slurred the word so badly it was barely recognizable.

He reached for his cell phone, but realized he was still in his underwear. "Beth, sweetie, go grab the wireless house phone from the bedroom. I need to call 911." He glanced at Jack who looked on the verge of hysterics. "Jack, run and get my jeans."

Beth hurried down the stairs and said into the phone, "Here's my dad." She handed the receiver to Jeff. "I already dialed."

Jack came racing back with the jeans, but Jeff held up a hand, signaling for him to slow down. With the phone tucked under his chin, he took the jeans from his son's hand and slipped them on.

Beth and Jack sat huddled on the steps as close as they could get to their mother.

"I don't..." Michelle tried to lift her head but groaned in pain.

"Don't move. We don't know if anything is broken."

Again, she tried to sit up.

"Michelle, stop trying to move." Jeff looked at the kids. "You both need to go get dressed for school."

"But Daddy," Beth whimpered. "We can't go to school."

Jeff reached out for his children's hands. "I know you are frightened. So am I. But I need to go to the hospital with your mother, and the best place for you to be—so your mother isn't worried about you—is at school. I promise if something happens, I will come and get you."

"But..." Tears filled Beth's eyes.

He pulled both kids into his arms. "We should pray. Dear Heavenly Father, we come to you this morning filled with fear for Michelle, Mom. Please touch her with your healing power. Please take our fear from us. We know You are in control." They could hear the sirens from Gamber Fire Department in the distance. "It won't be long."

Hearing the vehicle pull up, Jeff turned to go down the stairs.

Jack whispered, "Hallelujah."

Jeff stopped for a moment and looked at his son, in surprise. Leave it to Jack to remind him they were not alone. He half smiled and ruffled his son's hair. "You're right, buddy. Hallelujah." He gave each child a quick hug and repeated, "Go get dressed."

He quickly dashed to the door and was surprised to see his brother-in-law Blake who nodded, then flew to Michelle's side. "I heard it on my scanner and came right away. Michelle, can you open your eyes?"

Her eyelids barely flickered.

"Come on, Michelle, open your eyes. You can do it."

She slowly opened her eyes halfway, then shut them.

"Keep them open, if you can." Blake pulled his stethoscope from his bag. "I'm going to check you out."

She mumbled something no one could understand.

Blake chuckled. "I know you don't want me as your doctor." He patted her hand. "I promise not to look anywhere you and Annette wouldn't approve of."

The paramedics arrived a few minutes later. Jeff let them in.

They nodded at Blake. One said, "I thought that was your car."

Blake spoke again to Michelle, "The EMTs are here... my friends John and Matt. They're going to take good care of you."

John knelt beside Michelle. "How are you feeling?"

She mumbled something that sounded like, "Sore."

Blake explained the situation to the paramedics. "Slurred speech, heart rate thready, disoriented, no feeling on her right side. You can start the IV. We need to put her neck in a brace and move her on a board. Her left shoulder is dislocated. I don't feel anything broken, but I don't want to take a chance with her back and neck."

The other EMT, Matt, rushed out to get the board.

Blake looked over his shoulder at Jeff and said, "I can drop the kids off at my house on the way to the hospital."

Jeff nodded. "Thanks."

"What happened?" John asked.

"She fell down the steps." Jeff rubbed the back of his neck. "I shouldn't have let her get up alone."

Blake shook his head. "Jeff, this is not your fault."

"I'm supposed to be taking care of her."

"And you are. Have her legs gone numb before?"

"Once, around Christmas."

"What did her doctor say was the cause then?"

"A mini stroke."

Blake nodded. "I'm thinking that's what happened again."

Matt brought in the board.

John said to Blake and Jeff, "We could use your help getting her on the board with as little movement as possible."

John handed the neck brace to Blake, who carefully placed it on Michelle.

Beth gasped.

Blake looked up the stairs, noticing her for the first time. "Just a precaution, buttercup," he said. "We're going to take good care of your Mom. I promise."

They slowly lifted Michelle onto the board. Once she was strapped on, they lifted her to the stretcher.

The kids ran down the stairs behind them. "Can we say goodbye to her?" Beth asked.

The paramedic stopped. "Of course you can."

"Can we touch her?"

"Yes, but be very gentle," Blake cautioned.

Beth leaned over and kissed her mother's cheek. "I love you, Mom."

Michelle mumbled something.

Jack whispered in his Mom's ear, "Hallelujah."

Michelle gave him a half smile.

Jeff held her hand all the way to the ambulance. "I'll be right behind you, sweetheart. Don't worry about the k-kids." His voice broke. "They're going to Annette's." He leaned down, placing his head against hers, before softly kissing her. Jeff whispered, "I love you." His heart slammed against his chest as the EMT shut the ambulance door.

Then he hurried back into the house to help the kids get their bookbags. Reaching into his pocket, he handed each of them money for lunch.

Blake stopped him. "Annette is already packing them sandwiches."

Once the kids were settled into Blake's car, Jeff took off for the hospital.

He paced the waiting room for thirty minutes and was surprised when Blake arrived.

"Good morning, Dr. Anderson," the receptionist said.

"Morning, Amy." Blake came right over to Jeff. "I called Dr. Carson and he was already here doing rounds. He ordered an MRI. I'm going back to check on Michelle and will see if I can speed up the process of getting you back there."

Jeff nodded, and without taking his eyes off the double door he mumbled, "Thanks."

Blake patted him on the back. "Hang in there, buddy. God has this."

Jeff took a deep breath. He knew Blake was right, but at this moment fear was winning over faith.

He watched as Blake disappeared behind the very doors stopping him from going to his wife. He kicked an imaginary rock. How many times would he be forced to stand here and wait?

It was only a few minutes later before the receptionist told Jeff he could go on back.

Blake met him at Michelle's door. "They're prepping her for the MRI. I'm going to go make my rounds and will check back shortly."

Jeff shook his hand. "Thanks man, for everything."

Blake patted his back. "See you soon."

The MRI showed nothing was broken. Once they removed the neck brace and Michelle was off the board, the doctor re-located her shoulder. He told them she'd had a stroke, which was affecting the whole right side of her body.

Dr. Carson moved Jeff away from Michelle's bedside. "You need to prepare yourself for the end."

Jeff put his hand up. "No." He turned his back on the doctor.

"I know you keep hoping for a miracle, but as you can see... it's not happening."

Jeff held Michelle's hand in his. "Until she takes her last breath, there is still a chance."

The doctor looked at Blake, who had just returned. "Can't you talk some sense into him?"

Blake shook his head. "I'm praying for the same miracle."

"Am I to assume still nothing stronger than what I am already giving her?"

Michelle raised her left hand and groaned.

"That would be a no," Jeff said.

"I can release her to your care, but I've got to tell you, this time will not be as easy as the last time."

"I understand that."

"I can't say if the paralysis is permanent or temporary."

"I'll take care of her."

Dr. Carson shook his head. "I want to keep an eye on her for a couple more hours." He looked at his watch. "I'm going to finish my rounds and will check back. Then I'll decide if I will release her today." He looked at Blake and added, "Talk some sense into him." The doctor walked away, shaking his head.

By the time Dr. Carson returned, Michelle was sitting up talking, and Jeff was helping her sip a drink.

"Good to see the paralysis on your face is gone. Let's check out your arm and leg." There still was no feeling on her right side. "I know you want to go home, so I will release you, but I'm going to order a home nurse to come daily, and a physical therapist for twice a week." He looked at her seriously. "I know you don't want to hear this, but I have to be honest with you." He fiddled with the knot of his tie, looking down at his computer and said, "You don't have much time left."

Michelle looked at him for a few moments before reaching out and touching his arm with her left hand. "I know you think we're in denial about my condition. We aren't. Yes, we believe God will heal me. We also know He might not. It is His will, not ours. But I will not ever focus on the negative. I will live each hour I am granted, showing God and my family how much I love them." She pointed to her head. "This tumor will not defeat me."

Dr. Carson patted her hand. "You are a remarkable woman."

Jeff grinned. "That's an understatement."

Chapter 22

At the house, Jeff lifted Michelle from the truck into the padded seat of a wheelchair. He pushed her up the front walk to the steps leading into the house. At the first step, he tilted the chair back. Michelle groaned.

Jeff quickly righted the chair. "I'm sorry. Did that hurt?"

"A little."

"I'm sorry," he said again. He stepped around her and propped open the door, then gently lifted her from the chair and carried her inside. On the way to the family room, he stopped outside the guest room. "Do you want to lie down?"

"I've been laying all day."

"Are you hungry?"

She nibbled his lips. "Starving."

He grinned, before saying, "Not today dear, I have a headache."

Michelle tossed her head back laughing. "Believe it or not, today I don't." She laid her head on his shoulder. "For now I will settle for food."

Jeff put her down on the sofa. "I know you're ready for some hot tea." He stopped at the stove and turned the burner on under the teapot, then headed outside for her wheelchair. When he lifted it from the ground, he noticed the snow on the wheels, so he detoured through the garage and cleaned it off before taking it inside. By the time he was finished, he heard the kettle whistle.

While her tea was steeping, Jeff pushed the button to start the coffeemaker. "Man, I could use a good cup of coffee." From the refrigerator, he grabbed some butter and cheese. "Grilled cheese sound okay to you?"

"*Mmm...* my favorite."

He placed his hand over his heart. "I thought I was your favorite."

She laughed. "Don't make me laugh... it hurts."

When the tea was done, Jeff brought it to her, making sure to set the cup on her left side. She smiled at him. "You are my favorite."

He leaned down and kissed her. "You are mine, too."

"I know."

He laughed and hurried back to the stove to flip the grilled cheese. "Do you want to eat in there or here at the table?"

"The table would be easier, I think."

Jeff carried her to her spot before going back for the teacup. He clicked his heels and flipped the napkin open with a flourish. As he put it on her lap, he bowed and asked, "Can I get you anything else, madame? Soup?"

She tried not to laugh at him. "No, this is great." Michelle picked up half of the sandwich and took a bite.

Jeff patted her hand. "Nothing but the best for my girl." After they finished lunch, he glanced at the clock. "I'm going to call Debbie and see if she will get the kids from the bus."

"No, that will only frighten them. You need to be there to pick them up."

"I'm not leaving you alone."

She rolled her eyes at him. "And why not?"

He glanced at the wheelchair. "How can you even ask that?"

"Because you'll be gone less than five minutes. What do you think will happen in that amount of time? I will be fine." She winked at him. "I promise not to sneak out the back door and wheel off into the sunset while you're at the end of the driveway."

"That is a promise you can't keep."

She grabbed his hand. "When the time comes, it will come, and there is nothing we can do about it. What we can do is not dwell on it. I will be fine."

He knelt down beside her, taking her face in his hands. Tears stung his eyes. "I was so afraid I had lost you this morning."

"I know. But you didn't." She kissed him then said, "I'm here and the kids need to see you at the bus stop, to know that everything is okay."

He pulled her to him. She groaned. "Sorry, keep forgetting about the bruises. Do you need to lie down?"

"I don't want to be lying down when the kids get home. The sofa will be good."

He carried her back into the family room and gently put her down, propping the cushions around her. Suddenly he stood straight up, a big grin on his face. "I'll be right back." A few moments later, he came in carrying two fleece blankets. He laid them both on his recliner before scooping her up and moving her on top of them. "There, that ought to be more comfortable."

Michelle gasped in surprise. "You're letting me sit in your chair?"

He grinned. "Of course, it's the most comfortable seat in the house."

"So you say."

"And with those two stadium blankets, you'll feel like you're wrapped in a cocoon."

She tried not to laugh. He went out to the sunroom and came back with her Bible. Moving the end table to her left side, he brought the tea and the phone, placing them within easy reach. "There, you're all set. I'll be back in about five minutes."

"I'll be fine."

He leaned down and kissed the top of her head. "See you in a few."

"I'll be here, wrapped in my cocoon." She grinned.

Before it seemed any time had passed, the kids came running into the house. "Mommy." They rushed to her side, but Jack slid to a stop. "You're in Dad's chair."

"Amazing, huh?"

"Can we hug you?" Beth asked.

"Of course." She reached her left arm out to the kids. "I'm okay, just bruised." She laughed. "It's just another adventure in tumorville."

Jack danced around the room. "Hallelujah." He almost tripped over the wheelchair. "What's this for?"

"I can't move my right arm or leg, so I'm going to have to have a wheelchair, until the feeling comes back."

"What should I make for dinner?" Jeff asked.

"My mother called while you were getting the kids. She's bringing over dinner."

"Guess we better have our snack and go feed the horses before Grandma gets here." He tossed the kids an apple. "Better yet, we can eat on the way to the barn." He grabbed a couple extra for the horses. The kids reached for their jackets. "Beth, you want to stay in here with your mom?" he asked.

"Yes," Beth quickly answered.

"No, you go with them," Michelle insisted. "You need some fresh air after being in school all day. I'll be fine."

Jeff knelt down beside her. "Are you sure?"

"Yes." She pulled a blanket up to her neck. "I need a quick nap anyway."

"You need—"

"Go. I will be fine." She closed her eyes. "Go."

After they fed the horses, Jeff peeked in the door. "Mom's sleeping, so why don't you two stay out here and play for a while?"

Jack tapped Beth's arm. "You're it." He took off running.

"Hey, no fair." Beth chased after him.

Jeff entered the house through the garage. He took his tape measure from his toolbox, grabbed a pencil and the notepad he kept on a shelf by the door, and went to work figuring out what supplies he would need to make a ramp. He called Home Depot and placed the order with the Pro desk, then called Jason and asked him to pick it up on his way home.

He heard Michelle's parents' car pull up and went out to meet them. Before helping them carry the food into the house, he updated them on Michelle's condition.

The kids came running around the side and yelled, "Grandma, Grandpa." They ran up, throwing their arms around them.

"What's for dinner?" Jack asked, taking a bag from the back seat.

"Lasagna," Grandma answered.

"*Mmm...*" they all said at once.

"Mommy loves that," Beth said.

Grandma smiled. "Yes, I know."

Kay put the lasagna on the counter, before heading over to Michelle. She kissed her daughter's forehead and asked, "How are you feeling?"

"Like I've been run over by a truck."

Frank stood in front of Michelle, arms crossed. "Some crazy trick that you pulled, young lady."

"What trick?" Michelle questioned her father.

"Falling down the stairs just so you could sit in Jeff's chair."

Michelle giggled. "Hope my next trick is easier on the body."

Kay patted her husband on the back. "You are so silly. Dinner will be ready in about five minutes." She brushed hair from Michelle's forehead and asked, "Can I get you something to drink in the meantime?"

"I can wait."

Kay asked the kids to set the table while she cut the lasagna and tossed the salad. Jeff picked Michelle up and carried her to the table. As he set her down, the back of her shirt rose up.

Kay gasped, "Michelle," and rushed to her daughter's side. "Your back." She lifted the hem of the shirt, revealing the extent of her bruises. Kay choked on tears.

Frank came around and looked, too. He gave a low whistle. "You fell down the stairs on your back?"

Michelle nodded.

"Thank you, Jesus, for watching out for my baby girl," Frank said looking upward.

"Well, He didn't do a very good job."

"Beth," Michelle scolded.

"If He was watching out for you, you wouldn't have fallen down the stairs."

"I know when things are tough it's hard to keep believing that God is watching out for us. But He is."

Beth folded her arms across her chest. "Then why did you fall?"

"The problem wasn't with God. The problem was I didn't pay attention to what was happening."

"What do you mean?"

"When I got out of bed, I almost fell right away because my leg felt like it was asleep. When I got to the top of the stairs, I knew I needed to get your dad to help me, but I didn't want to wake him. All of these were hints telling me something wasn't right. Hints I ignored."

Jeff patted Michelle's hand. "When you got up, I saw you stumble and I told myself I would get up with you as soon as you came out of the bathroom, but I fell back to sleep." He looked at Beth. "You see, buttercup, God talks to us with gut feelings and we both ignored them. It's not God's fault. We just need to be better with listening."

They all sat down and Frank said the prayer. "Dear Heavenly Father, I thank you for your hand upon Michelle this morning. Please continue to touch her body and bring healing to her. Help us all be more aware of your voice. Bless this food we are about to eat. Amen."

Kay dished out the lasagna, then passed the salad and garlic bread. Jeff cut up Michelle's food and moved her tea to the left side of her plate.

Halfway through dinner, Jeff's brother Jason came in. "Pull up a chair, there's plenty," Jeff said.

"Smells good, but Heidi's expecting me."

"What are you doing here, Uncle Jason?" Jack asked. "You checking on Mom?"

Jason ruffled Jack's hair. "Here to drop some material off for your dad." He went around the table and gave Michelle a gentle hug. "Glad to see you home."

"Glad to be home."

Jeff excused himself. "Be back in a few minutes," he said and followed Jason. In no time, Jeff was back at the table.

"What's the material for?" Michelle asked.

"A ramp in the garage for you."

"Why? This paralysis is not permanent."

He patted her arm. "And the ramp is only temporary, too. When you're finished with the wheelchair, I'll put the steps back up."

"The perks of having a husband who is a carpenter," Frank said.

After dinner, Jeff carried Michelle back to his chair. Then the men and Jack went to work building the ramp. When they finished, Jeff put Jack in the wheelchair and dashed down the ramp.

"*Wheeee*," Jack laughed. "That was fun! Can we do it again?"

"Beth gets a turn first." Jeff took turns pushing the kids up and down the ramp, and he even gave Frank a turn.

Kay came to the door. "You guys are having way too much fun."

"You want a try, Grandma?"

"I think I prefer to have chocolate cake."

"Cake?" Jack and Beth ran into the kitchen, quickly followed by Jeff and Frank.

Jeff carried Michelle to the table. Putting her in her chair he whispered, "What a day."

"So, true." She gazed into his eyes. "From terrifying to joy in a single day. What a crazy life we live."

Chapter 23

Groggily, Michelle opened her eyes. She started to pull the covers off, but her right arm wouldn't move. The panic rose within before the memory of yesterday's fall came flowing back. She took a deep breath and filled her mind with hallelujahs.

Jeff leaned over and kissed her. "Morning, sunshine." He shuffled out of bed, came to her side, and lifted her into his arms. "Your chariot awaits."

She kissed his neck. "My knight in shining armor."

He carried her to the bathroom and sat her on the toilet, then pulled some toilet paper from the roll.

She held out her left hand. "I can do this myself."

He nodded. When she was finished, he helped her up, letting her use his body for support as she washed her hands and brushed her teeth left-handed. Then he carried her back to the bed.

"What do you want to wear today?"

"No jeans, that's for sure." She nodded toward her dresser. "Bottom drawer has my pants with elastic waistbands. I might even be able to pull them up myself."

He opened the drawer and pulled out the first pair, black with pink stars.

"The next drawer up has my t-shirts." Again he grabbed the first one. "No, not that one. It won't match thc pants."

Jeff held up a green striped tee and said, "Woman," rolling his eyes. "What are you talking about? Black goes with everything."

"But those pants have pink stars." She attempted to lift herself up, only to fall back down. "I know there's a pink shirt in there."

He dug around until he found it, and immediately turned toward her.

"I still need underwear and a bra. Top drawers."

"My favorite." He opened the next drawer up. "Does it matter what color?"

She laughed. "Only if we're having a date."

Jeff winked and said, "That could be arranged."

She put her hand to her head. "Not today, dear."

"Raincheck," he laughed.

"Definitely."

First, he helped her get dressed before pulling on a pair of his own jeans and grabbing a flannel shirt. Jeff carried her downstairs and put her in his chair again, then started the coffee and teakettle.

"Tonight before we go to bed, we'll have to set the coffee pot so it's made when you come down," Michelle suggested.

"You can do that?"

"Yes." Michelle rolled her eyes at him. "This is the twenty-first century, you know."

"Then why don't you?"

"Because I'm always down first and can easily make it before you get up."

Jeff grabbed their Bibles and together they read while the coffee brewed. When the teapot whistled he rose. "What should I fix for breakfast?"

"There's French toast in the freezer in the garage. Just grab a bag. You only have to microwave them for a few minutes to thaw them out."

Jeff came back with the bag. "What is all that other food in there?"

"It's for when I can't cook for you."

"But where did it all come from?"

"I just cooked an extra batch of every meal I fixed this year. One for us to eat right away and one for the freezer for when I'm not here. There are directions with each dish so you'll know exactly what to do."

"What do you mean... *when you aren't here*?"

"You know what I mean, Jeff."

He knelt down beside her, taking both hands into his. "Michelle, you will always be here. God will give us our miracle."

"If He doesn't..."

"He will."

"Jeff, you have to be prepared..."

"No, I will not have this discussion again. God will heal you."

She closed her eyes. "Jeff, just be prepared."

He kissed her and said, "I am." Then he stood up and stretched. "I need to get the kids up and moving."

Before heading off to school, Beth fixed Michelle's hair. Michelle hugged her daughter, kissed her cheek, and said, "See you after school."

Jack also gave her a hug and whispered, "Hallelujah," in her ear.

She whispered it back. It made her heart smile. "Have a great day at school."

Later that morning, the physical therapist arrived. "Hi, I'm Ashley." After talking for a few minutes, she lifted Michelle's right hand and asked, "Can you move your fingers?"

"No."

Ashley slowly moved her own fingers up Michelle's arm. "Let me know when and if you can feel my touch."

It wasn't until Ashley reached the top of her shoulder that Michelle said, "I can feel that."

"Great." Ashley repeated the process with Michelle's leg.

Michelle watched in dismay as Ashley moved along the bottom of her foot.

"Do you have any feelings on your right side at all?"

"Nothing from the neck down." She gave a heavy sigh.

Ashley nodded. "Okay, we're going to start with some passive exercise. Depending on how you do, when I come back in a couple of days, we'll be more aggressive. You will be able to do this yourself with your left hand." She looked at Jeff. "Or you can help her with these."

She quickly went to work on Michelle's arm and leg. "I'm not going to touch your back though. It's too bruised right now. I understand a nurse will be coming by later."

After Ashley left, Jeff asked, "How are you feeling?"

"Sort of glad I can't feel anything, cause I have a sense she gave me a good workout."

He laughed. "She sure did."

An hour later, the doorbell rang.

"That's probably the nurse," Jeff said, heading for the door. A few minutes later he returned. "Guess who your nurse is!" He waved his hand and said, "Ta-da," as Jennifer Carson followed him into the family room.

Michelle threw her left hand over her mouth. "Oh my gosh, how good to see you."

Jennifer gave Michelle a quick hug. "How's the headache?" she asked.

Michelle touched the side of her head. "You know, everything else hurts so much that the headache is sort of taking a backseat."

Jennifer put her bag on the table beside Michelle. "I'm going to check your vitals first, then..." She pulled out a needle.

"What's that for?" Michelle interrupted.

"For pain."

"Your husband knows I don't want—"

Jennifer patted her hand. "He told me to assure you this is not an opioid. It's just the strongest Ibuprofen he can prescribe. I'm giving it to you as a shot so it will work faster."

"Okay."

She gave Michelle the injection and said, "I'll be back tomorrow morning to check on you again."

Two days later, the swelling in Michelle's back had gone down and the feeling returned in her arm. When Ashley came later that day, she was impressed with Michelle's progress. But there was little headway with her leg.

Halfway through the first week, every little thing started to irritate Michelle. For a moment, fear blinded her. She couldn't get herself up, much less run outside. How would she handle the rage?

Panic blended with anger. The verse from Philippians quickly popped into her head. As the words filled her mind, she felt the anger fade away. Michelle quietly said a prayer of thanks for Miss Dorothy.

"Jen should be here any time," Michelle said. "Could you get a cup out so she can have coffee?"

Jeff grinned. "Already ahead of you." He pointed to the mug sitting on the counter. The doorbell rang and he went to let Jennifer in.

"Morning, Michelle," she said, leaning over to give her friend a hug. "How is everything going today? Any changes?"

"Unfortunately, I still can't move my leg." Michelle held up both hands. "But these work!"

Jeff handed Jennifer a cup of coffee and she took a sip.

"Would you l-ke a an-sh," Michelle's voice came out garbled.

Jennifer rushed to her side. "Michelle," she said, checking for pulse. "Can you smile for me?"

Only one side of her mouth curled up. Michelle reached up to touch her own face and slurred, "W-at ap-png?"

"Jeff, call 911," Jennifer ordered. He sprinted to the phone. "Tell them she's having a stroke."

While Jeff was on the phone, Jennifer called her husband.

"The ambulance is on its way."

Jeff rubbed his finger across Michelle's left hand, not knowing if she could feel it. He whispered, "I love you," equally unsure if she could hear him.

He lifted his head when Dr. Carson and Blake entered the ER exam room together. "I wish I had better news. The tumor has grown to twice its size and has caused her to have a massive stroke. I honestly don't know how she survived the pain this long."

Jeff squeezed Michelle's hand. "She will pull out of this."

Dr. Carson put his hand on Jeff's back. "I've told you before. You need to prepare for the end."

Jeff fell to his knees. "Please, God, place your healing hands upon Michelle."

Blake went to the other side of the bed and held Michelle's hand, joining Jeff in prayer.

Dr. Carson merely shook his head and backed out of the room.

"Your word says if we have as much faith as a grain of mustard, we can move mountains. Michelle has more faith than anyone I have ever met. She cannot ask for herself right now, so I am asking for her. Please heal her. In Jesus name, we pray. Amen."

Blake echoed the Amen.

A few minutes later, Dr. Carson returned. "It is in your wife's best interest for her to go to a nursing home."

Jeff stiffened as he spun to look at the doctor. "Never," he shouted.

"She's in a coma." Dr. Carson looked from her to Jeff.

"I realize that."

"She will need round the clock care."

"She is coming home." Jeff brushed the hair from his wife's face. "With me, where she b-belongs." He choked on the last word.

Dr. Carson slammed his laptop lid down. "I cannot force you, but I really think it's in her best interest."

Jeff pointed to himself and said, "I am what is best for her." He wiped his face with the back of his sleeve. "I vowed to take care of her. And I will."

"I really hope you will allow me to give her something stronger for the pain."

Michelle's hand flew up.

"Michelle," Jeff cried with hope. "Can you hear us?" There was no other sound or movement.

"It might have been an involuntary movement."

Jeff shook his head. "No, she has not completely left us." He bent over and kissed her. "I know you can hear us," he whispered in her ear. "I promise you will be coming home."

Dr. Carson laid his hand on Michelle's leg. "Then there is nothing we can do now, but wait."

"We can have faith."

Again, Dr. Carson shook his head.

Jeff settled Michelle in his favorite chair. He put some ice chips in her mouth. "We are going to get through this," he muttered, walking over to the French doors and opening them so the cold air blew in. "I wish you could see this. There are hundreds of green shoots pushing up through last night's snow. It won't be long before the tulips are in full bloom." He wiped a tear from his eye. "I would guess about two weeks."

He shut the door. "Maybe this afternoon if it warms up some, we can go out and sit for a little bit." He knelt on the floor beside Michelle, taking her hand in his. "Just wait until you see the tulips this year. You are going to love them. There's a big surprise waiting for you, so you hang in there." He put his arm across her and whispered, "I love you."

She laid there unmoving while he picked up her Bible, pulled up a kitchen chair beside her, and started to read.

The doorbell rang and he heard the door open. "It's just me," Kay called out.

His mother-in-law hurried to Michelle, leaned down, and kissed her forehead. "I know you," Kay said, squeezing Michelle's hand. "In no time, you'll be up cooking dinner. H-h-hallelujah." She choked on the word.

Jeff put his hand on Kay's back. "Our miracle will be coming soon."

"I hope you're right." She wiped the tears from her face and glanced at her watch. "Do you want me to get the kids?"

"Why don't you stay with Michelle? I'll get the kids so I can prepare them."

Jack and Beth ran into the house, but pulled up short when they saw their mother with her eyes closed. "It's like she's asleep," Kay said.

Jeff put his hands on their shoulders. "Go ahead and talk to her just like you do every day. Beth, if you want to brush her hair, I'm sure she would like that."

"Can she hear us?" Jack whispered.

"I think so." He nudged the kids forward. "Just tell her about your day."

The rest of the evening went by in a whirlwind of activity. A hospital bed was delivered and set up in the family room. Blake, Annette, and their kids came bringing pizza for dinner. Frank arrived with Hoffman's homemade ice cream for dessert.

When everyone sat down to eat, Beth looked at her mother laying in the hospital bed. "How is she going to eat?"

"She has a feeding tube in her stomach," Uncle Blake said.

All around the table, eyes glistened with tears. After dinner, Frank and Blake helped Jeff disassemble the bed from the guest room to make room for the hospital bed.

Together they rearranged other furniture to make a clear path to be able to roll the hospital bed from the family room into the guest room.

"Are you ready to move her in there now?" Frank asked.

Jeff looked over at his wife. Beth was brushing Michelle's hair and singing softly to her. Never had he felt so hopeless. "No. I think she would want to be out here with us until bedtime."

After everyone left and the kids were tucked in, Jeff pushed Michelle and the hospital bed into the guest room. First he undressed her, then put her nightgown on and got her comfortable before going to find his sleeping bag in the garage.

Putting it on the floor beside the bed, he knelt and prayed, "Please watch over our family while we sleep. I ask for Your healing. Please take this tumor from Michelle's brain, and until then, please give her relief from the pain." Silently he added, *Please give us the strength to handle whatever is ahead.*

Halfway through the night, he woke to what sounded like sobs. He jumped up to check on Michelle and found tears flowing down her cheeks.

"What is it, baby?" He gently wiped her face. "Are you in pain?" He started to reposition her and realized she was wet. "I'll be right back." He dashed out of the room, up the stairs, and into their bedroom, where he got her a clean change of clothes. He was back beside her within minutes. "We'll get you all cleaned up." He sweet talked her while he changed her nightgown. "There, doesn't that feel better?" He picked her up and said, "I'm just going to put you in my chair while I change the sheets." He kissed the top of her head and whispered, "I'll be right back."

After he stripped the bed, he tossed the linens along with her clothes into the washer before heading upstairs to look for another set of sheets. Finally, he was able to carry Michelle back to bed.

In the morning, the first thing Jeff did was change Michelle from her night clothes into every day clothes. "I know you are thinking, why don't you just leave me in my nightgown?" he said as he lifted her arms. "But I know how you hate to be seen in pajamas... so young lady, you are getting dressed." He lifted one leg and slipped it into the pants. "I assure you these pants match the shirt I picked out. They are plain black pants, so anything would go with them." He chuckled, "No pink flowers."

Once she was dressed, Jeff wheeled the bed into the kitchen. "I know you have taken a liking to my chair, but I do believe you'd be more comfortable in this fancy, schmancy bed." He quickly mixed up her formula and fed her through the tube before getting the kids up.

Beth hurried down the stairs, kissed her mother on the cheek, and started brushing her hair while Jeff scrambled up some eggs and made toast. Jack poured them each a glass of milk.

Joining the children at the table, Jeff sipped his coffee. "You two will have to walk to the bus this morning."

The children looked at their mother and nodded solemnly.

A few minutes later, the doorbell rang and the door opened. "Morning," Kay said.

"Grandma, what are you doing here?"

"It looks like rain, so I thought I would take you to the bus."

Jeff hugged her. "Thank you. There's plenty of eggs if you would like some."

"Thanks, but I had oatmeal before I came."

The small talk around the table was strained. When Jack started to get up, Jeff said, "I think we all ought to say a prayer for your mother before we start this day." The four of them prayed over Michelle, asking for healing and relief from her pain.

Beth hugged her mother and said, "I love you."

Jack kissed his mom's cheek and whispered, "Hallelujah." Before the word was even finished, he jumped back. "Hey, I think she tried to smile."

Jeff hugged both kids. "Have a great day at school."

Ten minutes later, Kay returned. "What can I do to help?" She looked around the kitchen.

Jeff had already cleaned up from breakfast. "At the moment, I can't think of anything."

"What about laundry?"

"I can do it."

"I know you can." Kay poured herself a cup of coffee. "But you cannot take care of Michelle, the kids, and do everything else by yourself."

"Why not?" He glanced at Michelle. "She does it every day."

"The situation is not the same. If that were you in that bed, I would be here helping her, too." He nodded. "Now about that laundry."

"It's mainly the sheets and her nightgowns from last night. They're still in the washer."

Kay shifted the laundry, then returned to the kitchen. "I'll be back in time to get the kids off the bus."

"Thank you."

"I believe Annette is making you guy's dinner."

"That isn't necessary."

Kay gave Jeff a look.

He said, "Follow me." They went out into the garage where Jeff opened the freezer. "Michelle has been cooking food for when she couldn't." He grabbed a foil pan. "Guess we will be having stuffed cabbages."

Kay took the pan from him and put it back on the freezer shelf. "Save this for another time and let Annette do this for you."

After Kay left, Jeff sat down beside Michelle, read the Bible, and prayed.

They fell into a routine. Jeff changed, bathed, and dressed Michelle. In the morning and evening, he would feed her through the tube. During the day, Jennifer would come by to check on her and feed her again. Ashley would come three times a week, working Michelle's muscles. Blake checked on Michelle daily. The rest of the family took turns going to the store, shuttling the kids to their activities and church, and doing whatever needed to be done to help. Dr. Carson also volunteered as a hospice doctor and stopped by to check on her weekly.

It was the second week when Miss Dorothy came to visit. She brought Jeff lunch and read to Michelle while he ate. She wiped a tear from her eye as she leaned down and kissed the top of Michelle's head.

"Thank you for coming," Jeff said. "I know Michelle loves your visits."

Miss Dorothy squeezed Jeff's hand. "I will see you next Friday."

It wasn't long before Dr. Carson arrived. He examined Michelle from head to toe. "You are doing a good job of keeping her free of bed sores."

"I keep moving her like you said."

"Have you noticed any changes?"

"She's gotten thinner, and it seems to cause her more pain when I move her."

Dr. Carson put his stethoscope back in his bag. "When was the last time you changed her?"

Jeff stepped back. "I change her every day."

"I'm not talking about her clothes. " He lifted the covers.

"Oh," Jeff said, realizing what the doctor was asking. "This morning when I got her ready for the day. Why?"

"Was she wet when you changed her this morning?"

Jeff thought about it. "Honestly, I don't know. I just changed her without thinking about it." He asked again, "Why?"

Dr. Carson looked at Michelle, then up at Jeff. "You have been doing a great job of keeping her dry." He lay his hand on Jeff's back. "That is the only reason I haven't put a catheter in her." He gently rolled Michelle to her side and patted the pad underneath. "It's dry." He lay her back down. "I need you to hear me. Her kidneys are shutting down and other organs will follow." He looked Jeff in the eyes. "I don't believe she will make it through the night."

The words shot through Jeff like a knife. For a second, he couldn't breathe. He collapsed onto the chair beside Michelle's bed. He closed his eyes, trying to shut out the words. When he opened them, he said with conviction, "No, you are wrong. God will grant us our miracle. I know it."

"Don't you think if He was... He would have already?"

"Everything is in His time, not ours."

Dr. Carson shook his head. "I don't believe in miracles. I believe in facts. And unfortunately, the facts are not in Michelle's favor."

"You know what Michelle would say to that."

Dr. Carson rolled his eyes. "She would say she would pray for me."

Jeff reached down and picked up Michelle's Bible. He opened it and took a piece of paper out. "This is her prayer list." He handed it to Dr. Carson while pointing to the doctor's name.

Dr. Carson looked shocked. "I... I thought she was joking."

"Michelle never jokes about prayer."

Dr. Carson handed the paper back to Jeff and continued to shake his head. "You can take me off that list. I don't need prayer."

"It's Michelle's list. She's the only one who can take you off it."

Dr. Carson mumbled something under his breath.

After the doctor left, Jeff took Michelle's hand in his. "Baby, he says you won't make it through the night." He placed her hand over his heart. "I can feel it right here. It's not true. There's no way you would miss tomorrow."

He pushed back his chair, knocking it over. With a laugh, he leaped into the air and clicked his heels together with arms spread wide. "Ta-da... tomorrow is Tulip of Love Day. Wait until I throw open the door. You and the kids will be amazed. This year God has outdone Himself with their vibrant colors. I can't w-wait for you to s-s-see them."

His eyes fell on his wife's deathly white face, shattering his fake happiness. He gripped the footboard of her bed. Was this what dying looked like? She hadn't made a sound or moved in days. *NO!* he silently screamed as grief knocked him to the floor.

Wet tears streamed down his face. He couldn't breathe. It wasn't supposed to be like this. He shook his fist at God. *You were supposed to heal her.*

Chapter 24

Jeff had a hard time sleeping. When he closed his eyes, he could hear Dr. Carson's voice saying, *"I don't believe she will make it through the night."* Jeff tried to follow that thought with, *'With God, all things are possible.'* He would drift off to sleep only to awaken to Michelle's rasping breathing. He repositioned her, making her more comfortable. Each time he would kiss her and affirm, "God is going to see us through this. I love you."

Never was Jeff so happy to see the morning sun. He reached up and touched Michelle's hand. "You did it. You made it through the night."

Humming a tune, he changed her and put her in a pretty nightgown. "We can't have you doing the tulip of love dance in a hospital gown now, can we?" He laughed. "It would be a pretty sight, you mooning us all."

Michelle just lay there. No sign of life other than her shallow breathing. He rolled the bed into the family room. After he fed her and got her settled, he poured himself a cup of coffee. Beth and Jack slowly inched their way into the kitchen, neither wanting to look at their mother.

Jeff smiled. "She's still with us."

Beth started to cry.

Jeff ran to her. "She's okay, buttercup."

"I was so afraid."

Jeff pulled both kids into his arms. "I know. So was I." He wiped tears from their faces. "No sad faces today. It's Tulip of Love Day!" He picked them up at once, one in each arm, and spun around the room until they were laughing. "That's better," he said. He put them down on the tile and prompted, "Now go see your mother. She's waiting for your hugs."

Jack ran faster and kissed her cheek first. "Guess what today is?" he said with a sly grin at his father. "It's Tulip of Love Day." He held Michelle's hand. "Woohoo, we get to have tulip tea."

Beth brushed and braided her mother's hair. When she was almost done, she ran from the room, then came back in a few minutes with a new hair tie. "Grandma and I found this at the store. It has a tulip on it with tiny little diamond rhinestones. You will love it." She finished the braid and secured it with the tulip tie.

"That is beautiful." Jeff gently squeezed Beth's shoulders. "I know she'll love it. Now, you two sit with your mother while I go change." He glanced at the French doors. "You know the rules... *no peeping*. We all look at once." He ruffled their hair and added, "I'll be back in just a few minutes."

Jeff ran up the stairs, grabbed the first pair of jeans from his drawer, and pulled a shirt from the closet. In the bathroom, he looked in the mirror. A pair of sad eyes stared back at him. Dark bags hung under them. He couldn't remember when he'd looked this bad.

He rubbed the overgrown whiskers on his face. When was the last time he'd shaved? He splashed water on his cheeks, picked up his razor, and tried to become someone his wife would recognize. When Michelle opened her eyes, he didn't want to frighten her. He dropped the razor. Who was he kidding? She wasn't going to open her eyes.

Jeff sank down to the floor. His heart exploded with grief as tears streamed down his face. He laid his head on his knees. His stomach and his head hurt so much he couldn't make himself get up.

All he could do was pray. "Dear God, please, I beg of You, don't take her from us. I—" He choked on his tears. "How do we live without her?" Sobs racked his body. "I can't do this."

Complete hopelessness overcame him. In his mind, he heard Michelle's voice, *"In our weakest moment, call on Jesus, He will see us through."*

He wiped his face, pulled himself up from the floor, and looked out the window. The tulips, glistening with dew, filled his heart with peace.

He leaned his head against the window and continued to pray. "Your word says, if you have as much faith as a grain of mustard, you can move mountains. Our mountain is the tumor slowly destroying Michelle's life. She is in so much pain she can't ask You herself. I don't even know if she can pray anymore. You know she loves You and has placed the love of Jesus in the hearts of her children, and in my heart. Without her, I don't know if I ever would have truly believed in You. Please God, I beg You to touch her brain and heal the tumor inside of her. I believe with all my heart that You are able. I know it's not my will, but Your will. I just don't know what I would do without her. My heart would break into a thousand pieces, but if it's Your will that she dies, then don't allow her to suffer any longer. I selfishly ask You to send a miracle to this house today, but if not, give us the strength to face life without her. "

"Daddy." The panic in Jack's voice returned the chill to Jeff's heart. He splashed water on his face again, now trying to hide his tears before opening the door. "Mommy can't breathe." Tears were streaming down the child's face.

Jeff dashed to the stairs, taking them two at a time. He was beside Michelle in mere seconds.

The gurgling sound coming from his wife stopped when he rolled her to her side and propped pillows behind her back. Jeff pulled the kids to him and whispered, "She's okay."

"She's dying, isn't she?" A river of tears streamed down Beth's face.

Jeff hugged her and Jack tightly. "We need to pray."

Jack pulled away. "We've *been* praying and God isn't listening."

"He is listening."

"Then why hasn't He healed her?"

"I don't know the answer to that. I do know that your mother is not dead yet, which means there's still hope."

Jeff lifted them one at a time to sit on the bed beside Michelle, then he knelt down in front of them, taking their hands in his. "We have always known there was the possibility of God saying no to our prayer. But until she takes her last breath, there is still a chance He will heal her. We cannot give up hope." He leaned down and kissed Michelle softly on her lips. The coldness of them shot hopelessness through him. He forced himself to say, "What do you think your mother would be saying to us right now?"

Beth put her hand on top of her mother's hand. "She would say you just need a little faith to move a mountain."

Jack put his fingers together. "Just this much faith." Then he wiped his eyes on the back of his sleeve. "I have that much."

"Me too," Beth said.

Jeff lifted them down from the bed and announced, "Go get your shoes and coats on." He forced himself to smile. "Today is Tulip of Love Day and we will not be sad today."

When the kids came back, Jeff wrapped Michelle in a blanket and picked her up. Together they walked to the door as if they were taking their final walk together.

"Jack, throw open the doors like your mother always does."

Jack took the handles of both French doors and pushed them open with a flourish. He flung his arms in the air and yelled, "It's Tulip of Love Day!"

Beth gasped. "Oh." She reached up and grasped her mother's hand. "Oh Mommy, if you could only see this. The whole bank is filled with tulips. From the top to the bottom, from one side to the other, all in different colors. It's like... it's like a rainbow of color everywhere."

Jack jumped up and down. "Daddy and I planted them after everyone was asleep."

"It is beautiful, isn't it?"

Beth started to cry.

"Why are you crying?" Jack asked.

"Because this was her dream and she can't see it."

Jeff lifted Michelle further up onto his shoulder so he could reach a hand out for Beth. "She might not be able to see it, but I believe she can still hear us, so we will tell her what we're seeing so she can see it, too."

Jeff started up the stone path to the center of the hill where the heart-shaped flower bed grew. He knelt down on the stone and reached out to pick the center flower. "This is the tulip that started it all." He lay it in her hand. "Who would have ever thought that God would use a simple tulip to bring two hearts together?" He kissed his wife gently on the lips. "I love you, Michelle."

It was barely a whisper, but they all heard it.

"Love," came out like a feather against Jeff's neck.

Michelle gasped for air and her mouth dropped open before he felt her go limp in his arms.

Jeff's heart splintered into a thousand shards of cut glass. He held Michelle tight, tears streaming down his face. "Please, God, no," he sobbed into her hair.

He barely felt Beth fall to the ground beside him. He had to be strong. The kids needed him. He fought the overwhelming grief and instead reached out his arm to pull Beth to his side.

Then he lifted his head. Where was Jack?

"She moved her hand," Jack shouted. "She moved her hand."

Jeff tried to find the words to tell Jack that he was just imagining it. His mother was gone.

Jumping up and down Jack hollered, "She opened her eyes!"

Jeff felt Michelle's eyelashes move like a butterfly kiss against his cheek.

Jack fell to the ground beside them, throwing his arms around them and almost knocking them over. Laughing, he hopped back up and shrieked, "She opened her eyes. Hallelujah!"

Michelle lay her hand on Beth's head and murmured, "Don't cry."

Beth jerked her head up. "Mommy?" The child touched her mother's hand on her own head and her face broke into a beaming smile.

"Michelle." Jeff hugged his wife tight against his chest.

"I c-can't... b-breathe," Michelle stammered, trying to untangle herself from Jeff and Beth. "Why are you c-crying?"

"We thought you were... d-dead," Jeff whispered.

"I'm not."

"I knew Jesus would heal you." Jack clapped his hands and started jumping again. "I *knew* it."

"He sure did," Michelle said.

Jack dropped down beside them, threw his arms around his family, and knocked everyone to the grassy ground.

Laughter flowed through the air. Jack was the first to stand, followed by Beth, and then Jeff, still clutching Michelle in his arms.

"You can put me down," she said, her voice now stronger.

"You don't have shoes on," Jeff said.

Michelle looked down at her bare feet. "Put me down anyway."

"You won't be able to stand on your own, so just hold onto me."

"Yes, I will," she insisted.

He cautiously put her down, at first clinging to support her weight.

Michelle stepped sturdily away from him, now twirling with both her hands in the air. At the top of her lungs, she shouted, "Hallelujah!"

"Maybe you shouldn't do that," Jeff cautioned.

She started to laugh. "I'm healed," she said. "I can do anything I want to."

She grabbed the hands of both children and started running around the tulips, almost tripping on her nightgown. She looked down at the flannel gown with red tulips on it.

"When did I get this?"

"Grandma and I went online and found it," Beth said. "Isn't it lovely?"

"I love it."

"Maybe we ought to go inside and get you some shoes. You don't want to catch a cold."

Michelle put her hands on her hips. "I don't think Jesus healed me only to let me get pneumonia. Do you?"

"Umm... No, I guess not."

She ran back to the red tulips, picked a handful, and tossed them into the air. "Thank you, God, for loving us and healing me."

Jack looked up at her with wide eyes. "Jesus answered our prayer, didn't He?"

"He sure did." She knelt down in front of Jack and again took his hands in hers. "Jesus touched my head and took the tumor."

"Did you feel it?" Jack asked.

Michelle nodded. She looked from one to the other. "I heard your father talking about the first tulip and I tried to say I love you."

"You did say *love*," Jeff said.

"I did."

"Yes, but then you gasped as if... as if you were taking your l-l-last breath." Beth looked ready to cry again.

"I thought so, too. But then I felt a gentle touch on my head and a warmth spread throughout my body. I heard Jesus telling me to open my eyes. So I did."

"You heard Jesus?" Jack giggled.

"Did you see Him?" Jeff asked.

"No, he was kneeling behind me." Michelle touched the top of her head. "He answered our prayers. The tumor is gone." She also started to giggle. "God is something else, isn't He? He brought us together with a single tulip and then He used our special day of love to heal me." She looked around the garden. "Sweetheart," she whispered. "It's *beautiful*."

"I couldn't let you die without your wish."

"I don't know how, but when you carried me out here I could see it."

Jeff pulled Jack to him. "He was my partner in this."

Michelle hugged them both. "It's so beautiful."

"And we didn't break the rules either," Jack said.

Michelle looked around her. "How is that possible?"

Jeff took her hands in his. "One tulip for each day, one for every hour we were blessed with you from March until October." He pulled her into his arms looking into her eyes. "That was our blessings to plant." He kissed her passionately. His heart swelled with love for her to the point he could barely breathe.

Beth and Jack started to giggle again, breaking the moment.

Michelle laid her head on Jeff's chest. She reached an arm out for the kids and the four of them stood in an embrace with the morning sun raining golden rays of warmth upon them.

Together they picked tulips, some for tea, and the rest for a bouquet for the table. Inside, Michelle put the water on to boil.

"Make enough for two more," Jeff said. "Your parents are coming for breakfast."

Michelle grinned. "Awesome." She looked down at her nightgown. "I better get dressed." Jeff followed her out of the room. When she started up the stairs, he took her by the arm. Michelle stopped. "Jeff, I can do this."

"You haven't been able to walk for three weeks. What if your legs are still weak?"

"They aren't." She took his face in her hands. "Jesus healed me from head to toe." She gave him a quick kiss.

"I know… it's just hard not to worry."

"Honestly, I feel better than I ever have. No aches, no pains, a perfect healing." She started up the stairs. Over her shoulder she called, "I think I hear the tea kettle about to whistle." She winked at him. "I'm trusting you to make the tulip tea."

He laughed. "One tulip petal, the rest water."

"Noooooooooo." Then she laughed. "Better have Beth do it." At the top of the stairs she called back, "I'll be down in a minute."

Jeff and Beth were in the middle of making the tulip tea when Kay and Frank arrived.

Kay took one look at the empty bed and all color drained from her face. Her legs buckled beneath her.

"No!" Kay cried. Frank caught her and together they collapsed to the floor.

Frank held her tight and buried his head in her hair. "I can't believe she's gone."

Jack ran to his grandparents. They both looked up. "She's not gone," he said and grabbed their hands. His excitement spilled out as he bounced up and down. "She's healed."

Kay glanced from one of them to the other. "What?"

"Mom, Dad," Michelle said, coming into the room.

They both spun around in stunned silence. Jack started hopping up and down once more. "Jesus healed her."

Michelle walked steadily to her parents.

Embracing her, they both kept saying, "Thank you, Jesus." Tears of joy flowed down their cheeks. Kay didn't want to let go.

Michelle finally pulled herself away. "Come see our garden of love."

She took her parents by the hands and led them to the still open French doors. "Isn't it breathtaking?"

"Did God do this?" Kay asked in awe.

"Yes," she grinned, "with the help of two angels, Jeff and Jack." She stared with them across the patio, then said, "I'm starving. What about you?"

Kay squeezed Michelle's hand. "I bet you are."

Michelle went to the stove where Jeff stood. She turned her back to the others and discreetly lifted her shirt, pointing to the feeding tube. "What is this?"

"A feeding tube."

"How long have I had it?"

"Two weeks."

"But why?"

"It was the only way I could feed you."

She hugged him. "Thank you for taking such good care of me."

He kissed the tip of her nose. "My pleasure." He put the bacon on the platter and took the tulip pancakes out of the oven. "Breakfast is ready." Together they carried the food to the table.

Michelle said grace. "Dear Heavenly Father, I come to you with a heart full of awe. This has been an eventful year, one full of tears and doubts and tons of faith, and now this wonderful miracle. Thank you, Jesus, for never leaving us, for loving us, and for blessing us, not only with the healing of my body, but the love each one of us share at this table. Continue to bless this family with your love. Hallelujah."

"Hallelujah," they all shouted at once.

Michelle wiped a tear from her cheek, then picked up the tulip teapot. Jack was the first to hold out his cup. She filled it only halfway before filling the other cups.

Jack poured honey into his tea, then passed the container to his grandfather. "You'll need a lot of this," he said with a grin.

They sat around the table laughing and eating. They were almost done when the doorbell rang. Jeff pushed his chair back and said, "That's probably Jennifer."

He let her in.

Jennifer adjusted the strap of her bag on her shoulder. Hesitantly she asked, "How is Michelle today?"

Jeff bit the inside of his cheeks, trying to hide his smile. "Come see for yourself."

They went into the kitchen. Jennifer's mouth flew open as Michelle stood up. "Would you like to join us for breakfast? There's more than enough."

"But..." Jennifer wiped tears from her cheek, "...we didn't think you would make it through the night."

"Jesus healed her," Beth and Jack shouted from the table.

Tears slid down her face as she hurried to her friend and embraced her. "I still..." she shook her head as if in disbelief. "I still need to check you out." Jennifer measured Michelle's blood pressure and temperature. "Everything is perfect. Have you called my husband yet?"

"We were going to do that after breakfast," Michelle said.

Jennifer pulled out her cell phone and dialed. "Honey," she said. "You are *not* going to believe this." She listened for a moment before handing the phone directly to Michelle.

"Hello, Dr. Carson."

There was silence on the other end.

"Dr. Carson, are you there?"

"Michelle?" Skepticism could be heard in his voice.

"Yes. Jesus answered our prayers. The tumor is gone."

"Impossible."

"I know it's hard to believe," Michelle said into the phone. "But it's true."

"Let me talk to Jennifer." Michelle handed the phone back.

"Yes... I know... it *is* a miracle... un-huh." A few minutes later Jennifer said, "He wants to see you in the ER immediately."

"Tell him we'll be there in about thirty minutes," Jeff said. "We're going to finish breakfast first."

Jeff grabbed another plate from the cabinet and filled it with tulip pancakes and some bacon while Michelle poured Jennifer a cup of tulip tea.

Tulip of Love Day had never seen such joy as was shared around the table that morning.

Dr. Carson stood waiting for them at the reception desk. His mouth flew open as he watched Michelle walking on her own two legs.

"I c-can't b-b-believe it," he stuttered.

Michelle grabbed his hands, smiling from ear to ear. "The tumor is gone."

Dr. Carson shook his head. "That's impossible."

"Everything is possible with God."

He pointed to the wheelchair, motioning for her to climb in.

"I don't need that," she said.

"Hospital rules," he insisted.

Reluctantly, she sat in the wheelchair. Dr. Carson pushed her into an ER exam room. "First things first," he said. "I'm going to examine you." He took her vitals.

"Doesn't a nurse normally do this?"

"I need to see for myself."

Michelle grinned. "Doubting Thomas."

"Who?"

Michelle and Jeff just grinned.

"I have you already scheduled for an MRI," he announced. "It will only be a few minutes before they come and get you."

"Great. Then you'll see the tumor is gone."

"We will see." Dr. Carson shook his head. He called for a nurse. "Let me know when they take her in for the MRI." Then he lowered his voice and added, "I want to be there."

Dr. Carson walked with them to the radiology department. He stood staring at the image of her brain as it appeared on the screen. Back in the ER, he pulled the scan up on his computer and continued staring at it without saying a word.

Jeff held Michelle's hand. "Is... is something wrong?"

Dr. Carson looked up at them. "It's impossible." He turned the computer monitor toward them. "Not only is there no sign of the tumor, there is not even evidence it was ever there." He pulled up another image. "This is the MRI we took two weeks ago, after you had your massive stroke."

Michelle jerked her head around to look at Jeff. "I had another stroke?"

"Yes," Jeff answered.

Dr. Carson pointed out places on the image. "You see this? That is scarring from each time you suffered a seizure or a stroke." He put the two images side by side. "You can see how different they are. On today's scan, there is no scarring, no sign of any trauma. It's... it's as if they aren't even the same brain. It's impossible."

"Not with God." Michelle couldn't contain her smile.

Dr. Carson closed his eyes. He took a deep breath before opening them again. "It is a miracle, isn't it?"

"Yes."

Dr. Carson looked down at his hands. He played with the screen of his laptop. "If someone yells at your Jesus," he frowned, "what happens to that person?"

"You yelled at Jesus?" Michelle looked from Jeff to Dr. Carson.

Dr. Carson looked sheepish. "Well, I was a little annoyed that you would have the audacity to put me on your prayer list."

"Why?"

"Being on a prayer list means you think something is wrong with me. And I would have assured you, there is nothing wrong with me."

"So that made you yell at Jesus?"

"Well, when I backed around in your driveway to leave yesterday, the sun was shining right over your house. It reminded me of a Christmas card of the manger scene. I looked up at the sky and I just got so mad that I shouted, '*Why couldn't You be real?*' " He rubbed the back of his neck. "Probably not my finest moment, but then I shook my fist at the sky and yelled, *'I don't believe in You, but these people do. If You're real, then prove it and heal her'.*"

"And he did," Michelle said with a grin. "He heard you."

The normally stoic doctor wiped his eyes. "I guess there is a God after all," he said. Dr. Carson looked from her to Jeff. "I deal in facts. And there is no denying the facts right here in front of me." He pointed to the two images and pronounced, "Jesus truly did heal you."

Michelle hopped down from the bed, throwing her arms around Dr. Carson. "I think God performed two miracles today—the healing of my body... and the healing of your heart."

Dr. Carson looked uncomfortable. Michelle turned before going back to the bed. She lifted her shirt and pointed to the feeding tube. "When can we remove this?"

"Right now," he said, and pushed the buzzer for a nurse. He shook his head some more and asked, "So how come Jesus didn't remove this Himself?"

"You still need to work, don't you?" Michelle laughed at the surprised look on Dr. Carson's face.

He chuckled. "Yes, I guess I do." The nurse came in wheeling a cart. Dr. Carson said to Michelle, "I want you to lay back, put your knees up, and relax. This will only take a minute."

The nurse handed him a stack of gauze. Within seconds, he had removed the tube.

"There, the final sign that there was anything wrong with you is now gone."

He stood up and started to leave. But then he stopped, took Michelle by the hand, and said, "Never in all my years of being a doctor have I ever seen anyone with as much faith as you two." He glanced over at Jeff. "I thought you were fools. But come to find out... I was the fool."

Jeff put his hand on Dr. Carson's back. "We are all fools at some point in time," he said. "What matters now is, what are you going to do with your newfound faith?"

Dr. Carson smiled. "I think I will be making my wife a very happy woman and joining her in church tomorrow."

Michelle swung her legs to the side of the bed. She looked at the computer screen where the image of her brain was still there. "We will be there also." Her heart swelled with joy.

She held out her hand to Jeff and repeated the verse they had said every day for a year. "*I will not die but live, and will proclaim what the LORD has done.*"

Jeff lifted her by the waist and held her up to God. "Hallelujah," they shouted together.

"Hallelujah," Dr. Carson said, closing his laptop. "Hallelujah, indeed."

The veil between dreams and reality began to lift. Jeff sank farther beneath the down comforter. He reached across the bed for his wife, but came up with a handful of air. He jolted fully awake. He was in his bed, not on the floor. *Michelle.* The joy of yesterday's miracle washed over him.

He jumped out of bed, pulled on his jeans, grabbed a shirt, and ran down the stairs, calling her name. The aroma of fresh coffee filled the empty kitchen. He wandered over to the open French doors and stepped out on the patio. In the center of the bank of tulips, was Michelle with her hands raised to the heavens. The sunlight radiated a path across the garden straight to her.

Joining her, he slipped his arms around her waist and kissed her softly on the neck. "Morning, sweetheart."

She leaned back into him. "The tulips are beautiful." Then she turned and wrapped both arms around his neck. "Thank you."

He kissed her softly on the lips. "You're welcome."

"I want to take a bouquet of them to church this morning. Let everyone see our tulips of love."

Suddenly the kids surrounded them. "Is it Tulip of Love Day again?" Jack asked.

"Every day is Tulip of Love Day now." Michelle grinned.

"God really did hear our prayers. Didn't He, Mom?" Jack grabbed his mother's hand.

"He certainly did."

"He must really love us." Beth reached down and picked a tulip.

"You know love is God's greatest miracle." Michelle lifted her hands into the air. "Can't you just feel the love He is pouring out around us?"

Jeff lifted her, holding her up to the heavens, shouting, "Hallelujah!"

Michelle threw her head back laughing. The kids danced around them, and in unison, they all sang, "Hallelujah."

Spiritual Hero

Miss Dorothy Lay

One person in every book I write will be based on one real person who comes from a small group of unique people who have touched not only my heart but my spirit. I call these people my Spiritual Heroes.

These people carry the love of Jesus so completely you cannot help but be drawn to them. When they entered my life I was truly blessed, and though many are no longer here on earth, their presence in my life remains a driving force in how I live.

In *Tulips of Love*, that person is Miss Dorothy Lay, the first Sunday school teacher I remember. I had some before her, but there was something special and still is about Miss Dorothy.

I was a very shy little girl, and going to a new church for the first time was traumatic. Miss Dorothy took the fears of a six year old and transformed them to feelings of being loved. Fifty-six years later, I am proud to call her my friend. Seeing her always puts a smile on my face and a song in my heart. Thank you, Miss Dorothy, for planting the first seeds of Jesus' love in my heart. You are truly my spiritual hero. I love you.

Other Books by this Author

"...page after page of inspiring words and photographs showing us how God uses nature to speak to us. A genuine treat for the eyes!"

~Loree Lough, best-selling author of 115 award-winning books

"The photographs and inspiring words of Vickie Fisher's HELLO GOD, ARE YOU THERE? filled my heart with joy and reminded me to look for the blessing of each day."

~Susan Meier, bestselling Harlequin author of A Father for Her Triplets

"...one of the strongest heroines, because she sticks to her moral code and religious beliefs in the face of her steaming hot love for Nick."

—Connie C. Scharon, Amazon best-selling author of *Enchanted Lover*

 After three long months in Mexico, PSA's top security agent Nicholas McFadden doesn't want another assignment. Then he hears her name – Brittany Fitzpatrick. Now he knows he can't refuse.

Ten years ago she almost made him believe in love, until she lied and nearly got him killed. Now PSA wants him to protect her from the very man who almost murdered them both. Can he trust her? Or is this just another evil plot by Vincent Capri to finish the job?

Contact the author at:

Vickiefisher.com
vickie.fisher@verizon.net

About the Author

Award-winning author Vickie Fisher lives on nineteen tranquil acres in Westminster, Maryland. She works for Amtrak as a chief entitlement clerk. In her spare time, she enjoys spending time with her children, grandchildren, family, and friends, who she believes are God's greatest gifts. When she isn't writing she is taking photographs of nature. Find more about Vickie at vickiefisher.com.